Sabrina
the teenage witch
the magic within
book 1

SABRINA THE TEENAGE WITCH: THE MAGIC WITHIN 1
Published by Archie Comic Publications, Inc.
325 Fayette Avenue, Mamaroneck, NY 10543-2318.

FIRST PRINTING.

ISBN: 978-1-936975-39-6

Printed in Canada.

PUBLISHER/CO-CEO: Jonathan Goldwater
CO-CEO: Nancy Silberkleit
PRESIDENT: Mike Pellerito
CO-PRESIDENT/EDITOR-IN-CHIEF: Victor Gorelick
CFO: William Mooar
SENIOR VICE PRESIDENT, SALES & BUSINESS DEVELOPMENT: Jim Sokolowski
SENIOR VICE PRESIDENT, PUBLISHING & OPERATIONS: Harold Buchholz
VICE PRESIDENT, SPECIAL PROJECTS: Steve Mooar
EXECUTIVE DIRECTOR OF EDITORIAL: Paul Kaminski
DIRECTOR OF MARKETING & PUBLICITY: Steven Scott
BOOK DESIGN: Duncan McLachlan
PRODUCTION MANAGER: Stephen Oswald
PRODUCTION: Vincent Lovallo, Kari Silbergleit, Rosario "Tito" Peña, Suzannah Rowntree
PRODUCTION INTERNS: Michael Crowe, Josh Kirschenbaum
EDITORIAL ASSISTANT/ PROOFREADER: Jamie Lee Rotante

FEATURING THE TALENTS OF:

Tania del Rio
STORY & PENCILS

Jim Amash
INKS

Jeff Powell
AND
Tania del Rio
LETTERS

Jason Jensen
COVER COLORS, RENDERING

Entering the Magic Realm

Introduction by Tania del Rio

Of all the characters in the Archie universe, Sabrina the Teenage Witch is probably the most versatile. Ever since her first incarnation by artist Dan DeCarlo and writer George Gladir, Sabrina has undergone many magical transformations. From a classic bob-haired vixen to a twiggy animated tween, to a live action TV-star, Sabrina has seamlessly kept up with her times.

I was fresh out of art school when Archie Comics asked me to give Sabrina yet another magical makeover. Naturally, I was both honored and thrilled to join the Archie team, and I was excited to take on the task of transforming Sabrina into a style completely new to Archie comics: manga.

The year was 2004, and it was the height of the manga boom in America. As a long time manga fan, my inspiration for Sabrina came from my favorite genres of this Japanese art form: Shoujo and Magical Girl manga, which are stories aimed at young girls filled with romance, adventure, and beautiful, strong-willed heroines. I recreated Sabrina and her world as an homage to some of my favorite Japanese comics including Peach Girl and Sailor Moon.

Fun fact: the first four pages of issue 1 are the same pages I initially pitched to Archie comics when I presented them with how I would change Sabrina's look and story. They liked it so much, they asked me to keep working on the rest of the issue and continue as writer and artist on Sabrina's monthly book!

What began as an experiment ended up as a successful 5-year run as, for the first time in her long history, Sabrina's comic went from containing short, standalone gag-based shorts to a serial format with a sweeping, dramatic storyline that spanned a total of 43 issues.

This volume collects the first 10 of those issues and, while each issue was intended to be able to be enjoyed on its own, the storyline begins to introduce threads that will become very important later on. Look carefully, and you'll see clues and foreshadowing hidden throughout. (Hint: Sabrina's encounter with the white fox in the 2nd issue, "Blue Ribbon Blues").

I hope you enjoy reading these issues as much as I did making them. Sabrina has been a good friend to me, even if she's been a little stubborn and selfish at times! But that's what I love most about her... she's flawed and acts just like a real teenager, with all the highs and lows. As you re-acquaint yourself with her manga persona, don't be surprised if you get swept away in her drama as well!

TANIA del Rio

Characters

SABRINA certainly has her hands full! Splitting her time between high school in the mortal realm and charm school in the Magic Realm is no easy task, especially when she has to juggle the interests of two boys! Sabrina is torn between Harvey's mortal charms and Shinji's magical variety. What's a teenage witch to do?

SALEM was once one of the most powerful wizards alive . . . so he tried to take over the world! The Magic Council punished him for his crimes by by imprisoning him in the body of a cat. He's pretty much harmless now, but he's always there for Sabrina when she needs advice or help!

Sabrina's aunts and legal guardians, **HILDA** and **ZELDA** are doing their best to raise Sabrina to be a capable young witch.

Sabrina's classmate at Greendale High and her major crush. **HARVEY** is a nice guy, but a little shy, and he's not sure how to act around the more outgoing (and unbeknownst to him, magical) Sabrina.

SHINJI is a young wizard with blue hair and a big attitude. He just started attending Greendale to learn more about mortals, and he's already made waves! Sabrina likes him a lot, but Shinji tends to play fast and loose with the rules, and she can't afford to get in trouble!

Sabrina's best friend also splits her time between realms. Though they attend the same charm school, **LLANDRA** goes to a private mortal high school. Lately, Llandra's been getting pretty close to Shinji . . . and Sabrina's not sure how to feel about that!

Chapter 1

Sabrina the teenage witch
IN
SPELLFREEZE
SCRIPT + PENCILS + LETTERS
TANIA DEL RIO
INKS
JIM AMASH
COLORS
JASON JENSEN
EDITOR
VICTOR GORELICK
EDITOR-IN-CHIEF
RICHARD GOLDWATER
VIDEO LAND

WHAT A GREAT MOVIE!
I MUST ADMIT, HARVEY, I WOULDN'T HAVE EXPECTED YOU TO PICK SUCH A CHICK-FLICK!
UH...ER, ACTUALLY IT WAS THE ONLY THING LEFT IN THE NEW RELEASE SECTION...
I GUESS YOU DO HAVE A ROMANTIC SIDE!
ANYWAY, IT'S GETTING AWFUL LATE AND WE HAVE SCHOOL TOMORROW!
I WISH I HAD A SPELL THAT WOULD SHOW ME HOW HARVEY REALLY FEELS ABOUT ME!
FIRST HE RENTS A ROMANTIC MOVIE AND THEN HE ACTS LIKE HE CAN'T WAIT FOR ME TO LEAVE!
TCH! BOYS!
'BRINA! DO YOU HAVE ANY IDEA WHAT TIME IT IS? IT'S A SCHOOL NIGHT!
ZAP
IT'S NOT THAT LATE!

HOW CAN MY AUNTS BE SO COOL SOMETIMES AND SUCH...SUCH...GROWN-UPS OTHER TIMES?
WELL, THEY HAVE BEEN AROUND A LONG TIME!
ZAP
YAWN! WELL, I'M READY FOR BED, SALEM. HOW ABOUT YOU?
UH...DON'T YOU HAVE SOME BIG REPORT THAT'S DUE TOMORROW?
OH, NO! I COMPLETELY FORGOT!
IT'S GOING TO BE A LONG NIGHT...
ZAP

TURN IN YOUR REPORTS, PLEASE!
YAWN
SABRINA, WHAT IS THIS? THIS ISN'T A REPORT ON EDGAR ALLEN POE!
APPARENTLY YOU DECIDED TO WRITE ABOUT "LUCKY CHARMS AND THE SPELLS THAT MAKE THEM WORK!" SABRINA, IS THIS YOUR IDEA OF A JOKE?
OH NO! I MIXED UP MY ASSIGNMENTS! I WAS SO TIRED LAST NIGHT I DID MY HOMEWORK FOR CHARM-SCHOOL, NOT MY MORTAL HIGH SCHOOL!
HA HA!
CHUCKLE
HA HA
ARE YOU... FEELING ALRIGHT, SABRINA?
HA HA HA!
HEH HEH
HOW MYSTERIOUS! LOOK AT HIS HAIR!
OOH!
NOW, LISTEN UP CLASS. WE HAVE A NEW STUDENT! HIS NAME IS SHINJI YAMAGI AND HE'S AN EXCHANGE STUDENT FROM... FROM...?
OH, WHERE I'M FROM ISN'T IMPORTANT!
OH, HOW EMBARRASSING! THIS HAS GOT TO BE A DREAM!
SHINJI! NOW I KNOW I'M DREAMING!
SABRINA... DO YOU KNOW HIM?
OH! UH, NOT EXACTLY....

RRRRRRIIIIIIIINGGGG!
SHINJI! WHAT ARE YOU DOING HERE? I THOUGHT YOU WENT TO CHARM-SCHOOL!
I DO, AND THAT'S WHY I'M HERE!
I'M DOING A PROJECT ON MORTALS AND HOW THEY LIVE WITHOUT MAGIC! I'M GOING TO BE SPENDING SOME TIME HERE TO GET A FIRSTHAND EXPERIENCE!
AND I WANT TO GET TO KNOW YOU BETTER, TOO!
WOW, HE'S EVEN CUTER IN THE DAYTIME!
BUT YOU KNOW, SHINJI, YOU HAVE TO BE VERY CAREFUL ABOUT NOT LETTING THE MORTALS SEE YOU USING MAGIC!
SEE? YOU DIDN'T BELIEVE ME, BUT THERE THEY ARE! THERE IS DEFINITELY SOMETHING BETWEEN THEM, DON'T YOU THINK?
I...DON'T KNOW WHAT TO THINK, AMY.

YUCK!
MORTALS ACTUALLY EAT THIS STUFF?
LATER THAT DAY
NOW THESE ACTUALLY LOOK EDIBLE!
ZAP
I'M SURE NO ONE WILL NOTICE IF I JUST "ZAP" A COUPLE EXTRA ONTO MY TRAY!
IT'S TOO MUCH WORK TO FIGURE OUT THESE MORTAL COMBINATION LOCKS.
ZAP
CLICK!
SAF-T
IT WOULDN'T HURT FOR ME TO JUST "ZAP" IT OPEN...
I'M ALREADY LATE FOR CLASS AND IT'LL TAKE FOREVER TO FIGHT THIS CROWD!
I'LL JUST USE A QUICK "ZAP" TO GET ME TO CLASS ON TIME...
MAN, THIS CLASS IS DULL. I BET EVEN SABRINA WOULDN'T MIND IF I ZAPPED THE CLOCK FORWARD AN HOUR!
ZAP

CONTINUE YOUR WARM-UPS FOR 10 MORE MINUTES!
CAN YOU STEAL THE BALL FROM ME, 'BRINA?
HA! OF COURSE I CAN!
OOF!
WATCH OUT!
HEH...

WHO DOES THIS GUY THINK HE IS?
HEADS UP, SHINJI!
GASP!
SHINJI!
WATCH OUT!

ZAP
scccreeeech!
SWOOSH
HUH?
SHINJI!
TWACK!
ARE YOU CRAZY?! WE'RE IN A CLASS FULL OF MORTALS! DON'T YOU REMEMBER WHAT I TOLD YOU ABOUT USING MAGIC?
IT WAS SELF-DEFENSE!
WHAT JUST HAPPENED?
YOU'RE LUCKY NO ONE SAW YOU, SHINJI! DON'T DO ANYTHING LIKE THAT AGAIN OR YOU'LL GET US BOTH IN TROUBLE!
DID I JUST SEE WHAT I THOUGHT I SAW? THERE'S SOMETHING ABOUT THAT SHINJI...
I'M NOT SURE WHAT, BUT THERE'S DEFINITELY SOMETHING...

SLAM
UH, HELLO... AMY, RIGHT?
LISTEN, SHINJI, LET ME GET STRAIGHT TO THE POINT. I KNOW YOU'RE HIDING SOME-THING!
I...I DON'T KNOW WHAT YOU'RE TALKING ABOUT!
REALLY? WELL, THEN YOU DON'T MIND IF I TELL EVERYONE IN SCHOOL WHAT I THINK. GOSSIP SPREADS LIKE WILDFIRE AROUND HERE!
LOOK, JUST TELL ME WHAT YOU WANT!
I JUST WANTED TO LET YOU KNOW THAT I THINK YOU AND SABRINA MAKE A REALLY CUTE COUPLE.
WHY ARE YOU TELLING ME THIS?
BECAUSE, SHINJI, I LOVE HARVEY. AND I KNOW HARVEY WOULD LOVE ME BACK IF SABRINA WASN'T IN THE PICTURE! SO, IF YOU LIKE SABRINA, WHY DON'T YOU JUST GO AHEAD AND DATE HER?
THAT WAY WE'LL BOTH HAVE WHAT WE WANT AND NO ONE WILL HAVE TO KNOW ABOUT YOUR SECRET.
IF I DO EVER DATE SABRINA, IT DEFINITELY WON'T BE BECAUSE YOU TOLD ME TO!
HE'S STUBBORN NOW, BUT AS LONG AS HE THINKS I KNOW WHAT HIS SECRET IS, HE'LL DO WHATEVER I WANT!
HMM...BUT I WONDER WHAT HE IS HIDING?

I'M TELLING YOU, LLANDRA, IT WAS SO MUCH EASIER WHEN SHINJI AND HARVEY WERE IN TWO SEPARATE REALMS!
NOW I CAN'T DECIDE WHICH ONE TO SPEND MY TIME WITH! THEY'RE BOTH SUCH NICE GUYS... AND CUTE,TOO!
WELL, CAN'T YOU ALL JUST HANG OUT TOGETHER?
GLAMGAL
THAT'S THE PROBLEM! FOR SOME REASON, HARVEY DOESN'T SEEM TO LIKE SHINJI VERY MUCH...
I WISH! LOOK, HARVEY KNOWS I LIKE HIM! IF HE LIKED ME BACK, HE WOULD HAVE ASKED ME TO BE HIS GIRLFRIEND.
BUT IF HE DID, YOU'D HAVE TO FORGET ABOUT SHINJI!
MAYBE HE'S JEALOUS!
AND THAT'S ANOTHER PROBLEM! I'M GETTING A MAJOR CRUSH ON SHINJI NOW THAT I'VE BEEN SPENDING MORE TIME WITH HIM...
SOMETIMES I'M GLAD I'M JUST A CAT! SOMETIMES I FORGET HOW COMPLICATED IT WAS TO BE HUMAN!
THE NEXT DAY...
WOW! THAT IS SO COOL, SHINJI! HOW DO YOU DO THAT?
MAGICIANS NEVER REVEAL THEIR SECRETS!
WELL, IF HE WANTS TO BE SO OBVIOUS ABOUT IT, LET HIM! I'M NOT GETTING INVOLVED!

DAY 2
IT'S JUST A TRICK, BUT IT ALMOST LOOKS LIKE REAL MAGIC!
DAY 3
I TOLD YOU HE WAS GOOD!
HE'S TALENTED, AND CUTE, TOO!
DAY 4
THAT'S IT! THIS HAS GOT TO STOP!
ARE YOU SURE YOU'RE NOT JUST JEALOUS THAT HE KEEPS SHOWING OFF FOR ALL THOSE GIRLS?
SALEM, I'M HARDLY JEALOUS! I'M JUST UPSET THAT HE'S BREAKING A MAJOR RULE IN MAGIC USE BY USING IT IN FRONT OF MORTALS!
AFTER SCHOOL Music Club
RIIIIGHT...BUT DON'T YOU USE MAGIC IN FRONT OF --
THAT'S DIFFERENT!
POW

HEY 'BRINA! HOW WAS SCHOOL?
BAD!
TV
BAD?
IS THERE A SPELL THAT CAN BLOCK OTHER PEOPLE'S SPELLS?
HMM...
WELL, TECHNICALLY, YES. IT'S CALLED SPELLFREEZE. BUT IT'S A VERY ADVANCED SPELL, SABRINA! ONLY FOR THE MOST SKILLED WIZARDS & WITCHES.
"SPELLFREEZE," HUH?
DON'T EVEN THINK ABOUT IT! LIKE I SAID, IT'S VERY DIFFICULT.
NOT ONLY THAT, BUT IF YOU'RE CAUGHT CASTING IT IN THE MAGIC REALM, YOU COULD GET IN BIG TROUBLE!
PEOPLE HAVE BEEN PUNISHED FOR USING IT UNLAWFULLY!
I SEE...
MAYBE IN THE MAGIC REALM YOU CAN GET IN TROUBLE. BUT THEY DIDN'T SAY ANYTHING ABOUT USING IT IN THE MORTAL WORLD!

HOW AM I GOING TO LEARN SPELLFREEZE? NONE OF MY CHARM SCHOOL TEACHERS WOULD EVER TEACH ME SUCH AN ADVANCED SPELL!
WELL, YOU HAVE ONE OF YOUR GREATEST TEACHERS RIGHT HERE!
YOU?
WELL, I WAS A WIZARD ONCE, YOU KNOW! AND SINCE I WAS PLOTTING TO TAKE OVER THE WORLD, SPELLFREEZE WAS AN ESSENTIAL SPELL TO MASTER!
I KNOW IT LIKE THE BACK OF MY PAW!
GREAT! TEACH ME HOW TO DO IT!
WELL...SINCE I CAN'T ACTUALLY CAST SPELLS ANYMORE, I CAN'T REALLY DEMONSTRATE IT...SO... IT WILL BE A LITTLE DIFFICULT...
YOU DON'T REMEMBER IT, DO YOU?
WELL IT HAS BEEN MANY YEARS...
THANKS FOR NOTHING.
HEY! I STILL KNOW WHERE YOU CAN FIND THE SPELL-BOOK WHICH CONTAINS THAT SPELL! OF COURSE...IT COULD BE A LITTLE DANGEROUS...
THEN WHAT ARE WE WAITING FOR? OFF TO THE MAGIC REALM WE GO!

MAYBE THIS ISN'T SUCH A GREAT IDEA AFTER ALL...
YOU DIDN'T TELL ME IT WAS BURIED IN A CREEPY, UNDERGROUND CRYPT!
LET ALONE ONE THAT HAPPENS TO BE HOME TO A VICIOUS BEAST...
YOU'RE NOT GETTING COLD FEET NOW, ARE YOU?
I ALREADY TOLD YOU THE BEAST AND ME ARE COOL! KAIBUSTU WAS GONNA LEAD MY ARMY OF HENCHMEN DURING MY BID FOR WORLD DOMINATION.
IF YOU SAY SO...
IT'S AWFUL QUIET IN HERE... MAYBE YOUR BEAST FRIEND DOESN'T LIVE HERE ANYMORE.
THERE IT IS! THE SPELLBOOK OF DARK AND DASTARDLY ARTS! JUST LIKE I REMEMBERED!
YOU WOULDN'T HAPPEN TO REMEMBER THE PAGE NUMBER, WOULD YOU?
RRRRGGGGGHH
WHAT WAS THAT?
JUST KEEP LOOKING!
WHO KNOWS WHAT ELSE MAY HAVE MOVED INTO THIS CRYPT IN THE LAST 100 YEARS!

I FOUND IT! NOW TO COPY IT DOWN...
WHO DARES TO ENTER MY CRYPT AND PLACE THEIR FILTHY HANDS UPON MY ANCIENT SPELLBOOK OF DARK AND DASTARDLY ARTS?
S-SALEM? TH-THIS IS YOUR OLD FRIEND, RIGHT?
KAIBUTSU! IT'S ME! YOUR OLD BUDDY!
I HAVE NO KINSHIP WITH ANY HOUSECATS!
YOU FORGOT YOU WERE A CAT AGAIN, DIDN'T YOU?
YOU? DO NOT MOCK ME! THE SALEM I REMEMBER WAS A POWERFUL AND MIGHTY WIZARD POISED TO TAKE OVER THE MAGIC REALM! YOU ARE JUST A STUFFED ANIMAL!
RRRRGGGGGHHH
UH, SABRINA- WE'D BETTER LEAVE!
I'M WAY AHEAD OF YOU, SALEM!
KRRRRSSH

THAT WAS A CLOSE ONE!
THE IMPORTANT THING IS, DID YOU MANAGE TO COPY DOWN THE SPELL?
I THINK SO...BUT I WAS RUSHED! I WON'T BE ABLE TO PRACTICE IT ON ANYONE, SO I'LL JUST HAVE TO HOPE IT WORKS WHEN I USE IT ON SHINJI!
POOF
THE NEXT DAY
THERE HE IS! IN THE ART ROOM AND SHOWING OFF AS USUAL. NOW'S MY CHANCE TO BLOCK HIS SPELLS AND TEACH HIM A LESSON!
OOH!!
HEH
NOW, LADIES, THIS NEXT TRICK I HAVE IS REALLY COOL!
READY?

MAHOU NO CHIKARA DE KATAMARE! *
WOW, SHINJI, YOU WEREN'T KIDDING WHEN YOU SAID THIS TRICK WAS COOL!
YEAH, THAT'S, LIKE, YOUR BEST TRICK YET!
OH, NO! I MUST HAVE DONE SOMETHING WRONG! THE SPELL WAS SUPPOSED TO FREEZE SHINJI'S SPELL, NOT HIS BODY!
RIIINNNG...
YOU CAN STOP DOING THAT NOW, SHINJI! IT'S TIME FOR CLASS!
YEAH, WE GOTTA GO! SEE YOU LATER!
MMPH!
* = "BY THE POWER OF MAGIC, BE FROZEN" - ED

SHINJI, CAN YOU HEAR ME? I'M SO SORRY! I DIDN'T MEAN FOR THIS TO HAPPEN!
MKAY, I... PR-MISE... NO..MRRE...SPELFF!
MOW...PREASE ...UMDO...ME!
OH, SHINJI, I DON'T KNOW HOW TO UNDO IT! BUT I'LL FIND A WAY! JUST...STAY HERE!
I DON'T REALLY HAVE MUCH OF A CHOICE...
LOOK, CLASS! SOMEONE LEFT THIS LOVELY STATUE FOR US TO SKETCH TODAY!
AUNTIES!
SABRINA! WHAT'S WRONG? WHY AREN'T YOU IN SCHOOL?
I MADE A BAD MISTAKE...

NOW YOU SEE WHY WE TOLD YOU NOT TO TRY AND USE THAT SPELL!
I KNOW YOUR INTENTIONS WERE GOOD, BUT WE'RE STILL DISAPPOINTED IN YOU!
I KNOW! LOOK, I'M SORRY. BUT CAN'T YOU JUST TELL ME HOW TO UNDO IT?
HEH.
THE ONLY THING THAT CAN MELT THIS ICE IS A KISS.
WHAT?
IT'S TRUE.
THEN CAN ONE OF YOU PLEASE COME BACK AND DO IT FOR ME?
WELL, SHINJI IS CUTE, BUT HE'S A FEW CENTURIES TOO YOUNG FOR ME!
SABRINA, SINCE YOU CAST THE SPELL, IT'S YOUR RESPONSIBILITY TO UNDO IT.
THIS IS SO EMBARRASSING!
HEY, IT MAY NOT BE SO BAD!
YEAH BUT IF HE'S FRIGID, DON'T TAKE IT PERSONALLY!
PAT PAT
GIGGLE
GIGGLE
THIS ISN'T FUNNY!

IT'S NIGHT-TIME AT LAST. I HOPE SHINJI'S ALRIGHT...
IT'S ALL LOCKED UP AND NO ONE SEEMS TO BE AROUND. I'LL JUST ZAP MYSELF INSIDE..
GREENDALE HIGH
SHINJI!
MRRRMPH! 'BRINA!
POOF
I'M SORRY I MADE YOU WAIT ALL DAY, BUT I COULDN'T RISK UNDOING THE SPELL DURING SCHOOL HOURS - SOMEONE MIGHT HAVE SEEN US!
...
YOU SEE, I HAVE TO... KISS YOU... TO UNDO IT.
TOO STUNNED TO SPEAK
I KNOW IT'S KIND OF WEIRD...BUT IT'S THE ONLY WAY. AND IT'S NOT LIKE IT MEANS ANYTHING... RIGHT?
MIGHT AS WELL GET IT OVER WITH.

IT WORKED!
ALRIGHT! THE ICE MELTED!
OKAY, I LEARNED MY LESSON.
LET'S NEVER TALK ABOUT THIS AGAIN!
DEAL!

Well, diary, I did it! I broke the spell on Shinji. he was blushing so hard, he could almost have melted the ice himself!
But I must admit...it was nice
...even if it didn't mean anything.
but what about Harvey? I've liked him ever since we were in middle school! the poor guy doesn't have any clue about the magic that Shinji and I have,,,, er, I mean, use.
Well, the important thing is, I learned my lesson. my aunts may seem young but they've been around way longer than I have and they're a lot wiser.
next time I better listen to what they say...
...and ignore Salem!
END

Chapter 2

Sabrina the teenage witch
サブリナ
BLUE RIBBON BLUES
SCRIPT, PENCILS, LETTERS TANIA DEL RIO
INKS JIM AMASH
COLORS JASON JENSEN
EDITOR VICTOR GORELICK
EDITOR-IN-CHIEF RICHARD GOLDWATER
GREENDALE
BLUE RIBBON
TOURNAMENT
HEY, GREENDALE! SUPPORT YOUR GREENDALE GROWLERS AS THEY TAKE ON ALL THE LOCAL SCHOOLS IN THE BIGGEST TOURNAMENT OF THE YEAR! DON'T FORGET YOUR BLUE RIBBONS -THIS SATURDAY AT GREENDALE HIGH!
SIGH... IT'S TIME FOR THE BLUE RIBBON TOURNAMENT ONCE AGAIN! AND THIS TIME IT'S EVEN BEING HELD HERE AT GREENDALE HIGH!
BLUE RIBBON
TOURNAMENT
Art Club
WHY DO YOU KEEP LOOKING AT THAT POSTER? IT'S JUST A BASKETBALL GAME!
IT'S NOT JUST A BASKETBALL GAME, SALEM!

IT'S A ROMANTIC TRADITION WHERE EACH MEMBER OF THE TEAM CHOOSES A GIRL TO WEAR A BLUE RIBBON IN HER HAIR TO CHEER THEM ON DURING THE TOURNAMENT!
MY LOVELY SABRINA! WILL YOU ADORN YOUR HAIR WITH THIS BLUE RIBBON AND THINK OF ME AS I FIGHT MY GLORIOUS BATTLE?
WHY, HARVEY! I THOUGHT YOU'D NEVER ASK!
AREN'T YOU GETTING A LITTLE CARRIED AWAY?
I GUESS YOU'RE RIGHT. THE TOURNAMENT'S ONLY 2 DAYS AWAY AND HARVEY STILL HASN'T ASKED ME TO WEAR HIS RIBBON!
FOR ALL I KNOW HE COULD HAVE ALREADY GIVEN IT TO SOMEONE ELSE!
I WONDER IF HE HAS ALREADY GIVEN HIS RIBBON AWAY... I'M SO STUPID FOR THINKING HE MIGHT HAVE CHOSEN ME.
HE DOESN'T SEE ME AS ANYTHING MORE THAN A FRIEND!
REMEMBER TO READ CHAPTERS 10-14!
HEY...UH, SABRINA.

OH SHOOT. I LEFT MY TEXTBOOK BEHIND!
Room 309
WHAT'S THIS?
SO, UH, MAYBE YOU COULD WEAR THIS FOR ME AT THE TOURNAMENT SATURDAY...
I'D LOVE TO!
I JUST THOUGHT I'D GIVE IT TO YOU BECAUSE I'VE KNOWN YOU FOR A LONG TIME...
THAT, AND YOU'RE MY BEST FRIEND THAT'S A GIRL.
GEE, HARVEY, HOW ROMANTIC...
I CAN'T BELIEVE IT! HE ACTUALLY GAVE IT TO ME! I CAN'T WAIT FOR THE TOURNAMENT!
LATER, 'BRINA.

WHAT ARE YOU GLOATING ABOUT?
WHA--?
SO, YOU THINK YOU'RE SPECIAL OR SOMETHING BECAUSE HARVEY ASKED YOU TO WEAR HIS RIBBON AS A LAST RESORT?
WHAT...WHAT DO YOU MEAN?
ISN'T IT OBVIOUS? WHY ELSE WOULD HARVEY HAVE WAITED UNTIL THE LAST MINUTE TO ASK YOU?
WELL, IT'S NONE OF YOUR BUSINESS. I'M SURE THERE'S A GOOD REASON HE WAITED UNTIL NOW TO ASK ME.
OF COURSE. AFTER ALL, HE ALREADY OFFERED THE RIBBON TO ME.
HE...HE DID?
THAT'S RIGHT. AND I TURNED HIM DOWN BECAUSE FIVE OTHER GUYS ALREADY ASKED ME FIRST!
LIKE I CARE ANYWAY! IT'S YOUR LOSS!

CHARM SCHOOL - THE MAGIC REALM
YOU NEVER TOLD ME HOW HARD IT WOULD BE TO GO TO TWO SCHOOLS, 'BRINA!
IF I HAD KNOWN, I WOULD HAVE THOUGHT TWICE BEFORE ENROLLING IN YOUR MORTAL HIGH SCHOOL!
OH STOP COMPLAINING, SHINJI.
IF ME AND SABRINA CAN HANDLE IT, SO CAN YOU!
ARE YOU OKAY, SABRINA? YOU SEEM DOWN TONIGHT.
IT'S NOTHING...I'M JUST TIRED.
OKAY, CLASS, I HAVE SOME EXCITING NEWS SO LISTEN UP! AS YOU KNOW, YOU ARE NOW IN YOUR SOPHOMORE YEAR OF CHARM SCHOOL.
THEREFORE IT IS TIME TO COMPLETE ONE OF THE MOST IMPORTANT STEPS IN YOUR LIFE AS A WITCH OR WIZARD!
OH, NO!
NOT A STANDARDIZED TEST! PLEASE, PROFESSOR LUNATA, ANYTHING BUT THAT!
WELL, SOME MIGHT CALL IT A TEST, BUT IT'S ACTUALLY AN ENJOYABLE TASK.
THE TIME HAS COME FOR YOU TO MAKE YOUR OWN FLYING BROOM-STICKS!
OOH!
FINALLY!
COOL!

NOW, IT'S IMPORTANT TO KNOW THAT MAKING BROOMS IS AN ANCIENT ART AND IT MUST BE DONE ACCORDING TO A STRICT SET OF GUIDELINES!
THE FIRST AND MOST IMPORTANT STEP IS GATHERING YOUR MATERIALS FOR THE BROOM. THIS MUST BE DONE UNDER THE LIGHT OF A FULL MOON!
THE NEXT FULL MOON IS ON SATURDAY NIGHT, SO I AM AFRAID WE WILL NEED TO HAVE AN EXTRA CLASS THAT NIGHT. WE SIMPLY CAN'T AFFORD TO WAIT ANOTHER MONTH.
OH, NO!
IS THERE A PROBLEM, SABRINA?
I JUST... I HAD MADE OTHER PLANS FOR SATURDAY...
WELL, I AM VERY SORRY, SABRINA. BUT THIS CLASS IS MANDATORY. DON'T WORRY THOUGH; YOU WILL RECEIVE EXTRA CREDIT!
I DON'T WANT EXTRA CREDIT! I WANT TO GO TO HARVEY'S GAME!
I'M REALLY SORRY, HARVEY!
IT'S FINE. WHATEVER. YOU HAVE OTHER THINGS TO DO.
IT'S NOT MY CHOICE! I REALLY WISH IT DIDN'T HAPPEN THIS WAY...
HERE, HARVEY. MAYBE YOU CAN FIND SOMEONE WHO CAN WEAR IT FOR YOU.
KEEP IT. I DON'T KNOW WHO ELSE I'D ASK ANYWAY.
I'LL TRY TO GET BACK BEFORE THE GAME ENDS, HARVEY! I'LL STILL CHEER YOU ON!

I'M SURE YOU'VE ALL HEARD OF MAGICAL FORESTS LIKE THIS ONE HERE. THEY'RE SO FULL OF MAGICAL ENERGY THAT YOUR OWN MAGIC WILL ESSENTIALLY BE SMOTHERED.
THAT MEANS YOU'LL BE GATHERING MATERIALS FOR YOUR BROOMS WITHOUT THE AID OF MAGIC!
GROAN
SINCE YOU WON'T HAVE MAGIC YOU'LL NEED TO TRAVEL IN GROUPS. DON'T GO TOO DEEP INTO THE FOREST!
NO MAGIC?!
IT'S GONNA TAKE FOREVER!
DANGEROUS THINGS SOMETIMES DWELL THERE. IN FACT, I BETTER WARN YOU ABOUT SOME OF THE THINGS YOU MAY FIND SUCH AS...
THE FIRST ROUND OF THE TOURNAMENT WILL BE ENDING SOON. IF HARVEY'S TEAM DID OKAY, THEY'LL BE ADVANCING TO THE FINALS!
ONCE IN THE FOREST, YOU MUST GATHER SEVERAL ESSENTIAL INGREDIENTS.
YOU WILL NEED A STICK OF WOOD FOR YOUR HANDLE,
A TYPE OF PLANT FOR YOUR BINDINGS,
AND SOMETHING SPECIAL TO ADD THE ELEMENT OF FLIGHT.
SOMETHING SPECIAL? LIKE WHAT?
I WAS BEING PURPOSEFULLY VAGUE. WHAT YOU CHOOSE WILL GIVE PERSONALITY TO YOUR BROOM AND MAKE IT YOUR OWN!
LASTLY, YOU WILL NEED A GIFT OF A STRAND OF HAIR! IT MUST BE A GIFT! IT CAN NOT BE YOUR OWN AND IT CAN NOT BE STOLEN!
HAIR?!
GROSS!
I DON'T WANT TO TOUCH ANYONE'S HAIR!
NOW, NOW! YOU ALL KNOW EVERY WITCHING SPELL MUST CONTAIN AT LEAST ONE NASTY INGREDIENT!
YOU CAN HAVE THIS STRAND OF MY HAIR, LLANDRA!
EW! GROSS! I DON'T WANT YOUR HAIR!
YEAH, SHE ACTUALLY WANTS HER BROOM TO WORK, SHINJI!

I CAN HELP YOU GUYS FIND THE BEST WOOD AND PLANTS FOR YOUR BROOMS.
MY FATHER TAUGHT ME EVERYTHING THERE IS TO KNOW ABOUT THE MAGIC OF PLANTS.
AFTER ALL, HE IS A SHAMAN FROM THE BRAZILIAN RAINFORESTS!
BUT WHAT ABOUT THE HAIR?
WHERE ON EARTH ARE WE SUPPOSED TO GET A GIFT OF HAIR?!
I HOPE I GET A HAIR FROM A SILVER UNICORN! I BET THEY LIVE DEEP IN MAGICAL FORESTS LIKE THIS ONE!
UH... I DON'T THINK THAT'S GOING TO HAPPEN.
I JUST HOPE WE DON'T GET ANY HAIRS FROM THE GIANT TARANTULAS THAT LIVE HERE!
OOOH! HERE'S SOME GOOD STUFF! THEY SAY WILLOW-TAIL MAKES YOUR BROOMS FASTER...
AH! BUT SPONGE-TUFTS GIVE IT MORE OF A BOUNCE... IT'S GOING TO BE SO HARD TO CHOOSE...
DONE AND DONE!
SABRINA! YOU CAN'T RUSH SOMETHING LIKE THIS!
THE BROOM YOU MAKE TONIGHT YOU'LL HAVE FOR THE REST OF YOUR LIFE!
YOU SURE SEEM EAGER TO GET BACK TO THE MORTAL WORLD. TO HARVEY.

YOU WOULDN'T UNDERSTAND, SHINJI.
STOP BICKERING, GUYS! LOOK OVER HERE--I FOUND A GREAT PLANT!
I WONDER HOW HARVEY'S DOING...
ALRIGHT! WE MADE IT TO THE FINAL ROUND!
YEAH!
I WONDER HOW SABRINA'S DOING...
SIGH...
MY RIBBON!

HOLD ON GUYS, I'LL BE RIGHT BACK!
OUCH!
IF ONLY I COULD USE MAGIC TO GET IT BACK!
PHEW! I MAY MISS HARVEY'S GAME BUT I'D NEVER FORGIVE MYSELF IF I LOST THIS!
THIS FOG! WHERE DID IT COME FROM? I CAN'T SEE ANYTHING!
LLANDRA! SHINJI! CAN YOU HEAR ME?
I DIDN'T GO THAT FAR, DID I?! WHY CAN'T THEY HEAR ME?
IT'S LIKE MY VOICE IS BEING SUCKED INTO THE FOG!
NOW...
...I'LL NEVER MAKE IT BACK IN TIME TO SEE HARVEY PLAY!

A WATERFALL?! NOW I REALLY AM LOST.
WHAT SHOULD I DO?
EXCUSE ME.
OH! I'M SORRY! I DIDN'T THINK YOU WERE...UM...ALIVE.
OF COURSE I'M ALIVE. WE ROCKS HAVE BEEN HERE LONGER THAN THE FOREST ITSELF!
YOU WOULDN'T KNOW THE WAY OUT OF THE FOREST...WOULD YOU?
OF COURSE I DO. ROCKS ARE ALL-KNOWING AND WISE. BUT BEFORE I CAN TELL YOU, YOU MUST ANSWER MY RIDDLE!
WELL, I'M IN A BIT OF A RUSH... BUT I GUESS I HAVE NO OTHER CHOICE.
AHEM! WHAT WALKS ON AIR, SWIMS ON LAND AND FLIES IN- WAIT...THAT ISN'T RIGHT. LET ME START OVER.
WHAT FLIES ON LAND, WALKS ON WATER AND... NO, THAT ISN'T IT EITHER.
IT'S BEEN SUCH A LONG TIME SINCE I'VE SAID THIS RIDDLE! LET ME CONCENTRATE...
HRM...
...
ZZZZZZZZZZZZ
WHAT THE--! HE FELL ASLEEP!
DIDN'T YOUR TEACHER TELL YOU THAT IT'S POINTLESS TO TALK TO ROCKS?

SMIRK
WHO ARE YOU? WHAT ARE YOU DOING ALONE IN THE FOREST?! IT'S DANGEROUS FOR A LITTLE KID LIKE YOU!
MY NAME'S KIT AND I LIVE HERE.
HE MUST BE A FOREST SPRITE!
HOW CUTE!
ARE YOU LOST?
YES I AM! CAN YOU HELP ME GET OUT OF HERE?
SURE. BUT FIRST I NEED YOU TO HELP ME!
THERE'S ALWAYS A CATCH...
OKAY, WHAT DO YOU WANT?
SNIFF-
I LOST MY TREASURE DOWN A HOLE AND MY ARMS ARE TOO SHORT TO REACH IT!
COME WITH ME, I'LL SHOW YOU!

SEE? I CAN'T REACH! IF YOU GET IT OUT FOR ME, I'LL HELP YOU FIND YOUR WAY OUT OF THE FOREST!
IT'S A DEAL.
OH, NO! MY ARMS DON'T REACH EITHER! SILLY KID, WHY'D YOU STICK IT ALL THE WAY DOWN THERE? IF I COULD ONLY USE MAGIC, I'D HAVE IT OUT IN NO TIME!
SNIFFLE...I WAS TRYING TO BE LIKE A SQUIRREL! WHAT AM I GOING TO DO?
DON'T CRY. WE'LL FIGURE SOMETHING OUT. NOW, IF WE JUST HAD A PIECE OF STRING OR...
I KNOW!
THE RIBBON HARVEY GAVE ME... I CAN USE THIS!
I WONDER HOW HARVEY'S DOING RIGHT NOW...
LET'S SEE IF THIS WORKS, OKAY?
OOH

PLEASE WORK! I WANT TO HURRY BACK... I WANT TO SEE HARVEY'S GAME!
YES!
BZZZZZZZZZZZ
I DID IT! IF ONLY SABRINA COULD SEE ME NOW...
THAT WAS UNBELIEVABLE, HARVEY! AND RIGHT BEFORE HALFTIME, TOO!
DARN!
GROWLERS
I GUESS I JUST GOT A BIT OF LUCK!
YOU DID IT!
I GUESS I JUST GOT A BIT OF LUCK!
GROWLERS 21

SO...WHAT IS IT?
IT'S AN ANCIENT MEDALLION.
IT HOLDS THE ESSENCE OF THE FOREST...
IT HAS AMAZING POWERS!
COOL, HUH?
REALLY?!
NAH. I JUST GOT IT IN MY CEREAL BOX!
KRISPY KRUNCH!
WHAT?! YOU MADE ME GO THROUGH ALL THAT TROUBLE FOR A CEREAL BOX PRIZE?!
HEE HEE HEE!
FINE. WHATEVER. NOW IT'S YOUR TURN TO HELP ME!
SILLY GIRL!
FSSSSHH
DIDN'T YOUR TEACHER WARN YOU ABOUT TALKING TO FOX SPIRITS?
WHAT?!!
HEH HEH!
HEY! COME BACK, YOU CHEATER!

I SHOULD HAVE LISTENED TO PROFESSOR LUNATA'S WARNINGS!
YOU THINK YOU CAN GET AWAY SO EASY?! YOU WASTED MY TIME!
THANKS TO YOU I'M GONNA MISS HARVEY'S GAME!
GRAB
OOF!
BY THE WAY...THAT'S A GIFT.
HIS HAIR!
WAIT! DON'T LEAVE ME HERE!
SABRINA? IS THAT YOU?
HUH?

SABRINA! YOU'RE OKAY!
THAT CRAZY FOX LED ME OUT OF THE FOREST AFTER ALL!
WE WERE SO WORRIED ABOUT YOU!
I GOT A CROW FEATHER! IT'S NOT TECHNICALLY A HAIR, BUT PROFESSOR LUNATA SAYS IT'LL STILL WORK!
I FOUND A FOREST PIXIE WHO WAS BRUSHING HER HAIR! SHE GAVE ME ONE OF HERS TO KEEP!
WHAT DID YOU GET, SHINJI?
— WELL.. LET'S JUST SAY IT WASN'T WHAT I WAS HOPING FOR...
AND WHAT DID YOU RECEIVE, SABRINA?
OH...I RAN INTO A WHITE FOX SPIRIT. HE TRICKED ME, BUT HE GAVE ME ONE OF HIS HAIRS...
IMPRESSIVE, SABRINA! FOREST TRICKSTERS USUALLY DON'T LIKE TO HELP ANYONE OUT! ESPECIALLY FOXES!
I GUESS...
I BET HARVEY'S GAME IS ALMOST OVER... I HOPE HE'S NOT TOO MAD AT ME.

WHAT'S WRONG, SABRINA? THIS SHOULD BE A HAPPY EVENT.
I KNOW... BUT I CAN'T HELP BUT FEEL UPSET BECAUSE I LET A FRIEND DOWN TODAY.
HMM...
I SEE. WELL, SABRINA, WHY DON'T WE MAKE YOUR BROOM FIRST?
IT CAN BE A DEMONSTRATION FOR THE REST OF THE CLASS.
NOW, CLASS, PAY ATTENTION TO THE WAY WE MIX OUR INGREDIENTS!
NOW THAT WE ARE OUTSIDE THE FOREST, YOU'LL BE ABLE TO USE MAGIC AGAIN!
WE HAVE A STICK OF HONEYWOOD... A SPRIG OF FERNLILLY... AND A HAIR OF FOX-
-WHICH, BY THE WAY, WILL ADD QUITE A BIT OF PERSONALITY TO YOUR BROOM, SABRINA!
YOU'LL HAVE TO BE CAREFUL WITH THIS BROOM AS IT WILL BE APT TO CAUSE A LITTLE MISCHIEF AS WELL!
FSSSSSSSHH
LASTLY, WE NEED SOMETHING SPECIAL!
OH, NO! I FORGOT TO LOOK FOR SOMETHING SPECIAL WHILE I WAS IN THE FOREST!

HEY, SABRINA!
YEAH, I KNOW I WASN'T USING MY BRAIN, SHINJI! BUT I WAS A LITTLE PREOCCUPIED!
NO, SABRINA! YOUR RIBBON!
OHHH! MY RIBBON! OF COURSE! THIS IS SOMETHING SPECIAL!
ALRIGHT, LET'S MAKE YOUR BROOM, SABRINA! FOLLOW MY LEAD!
MAHOU-NO-HOUKI!

COOL!
WOW!!
OOH!
CONGRATULATIONS, SABRINA! YOUR VERY FIRST MAGICAL BROOM! MAY IT LAST FOR A LONG, LONG TIME!
THANKS, PROFESSOR LUNATA.
YAY, 'BRINA!
NOW, GO ON.
WHAT? WHAT DO YOU MEAN?
YOU HAVE SOMEWHERE YOU NEED TO BE, RIGHT? SO HOP ON AND GET THERE BEFORE IT'S TOO LATE!
BUT...BUT I HAVEN'T BEEN TRAINED ON HOW TO RIDE A BROOM! I HAVEN'T GOTTEN MY LICENSE YET!
WELL, JUST THIS ONCE, I'LL HELP YOU OUT WITH A LITTLE SPELL. IT OUGHT TO KEEP YOUR BROOM UNDER CONTROL UNTIL TOMORROW.
BUT DON'T TRY RIDING IT AGAIN UNTIL OUR NEXT CLASS!
YIKES! TH-THANK YOU, PROFESSOR LUNATA!
FOOSH!

WOW! I CAN'T WAIT TO RIDE MINE!
NO FAIR!
HEY, PROF! CAN I GO HOME EARLY, TOO?
NOT UNTIL YOU MAKE YOUR BROOM, MR. YAMAGI!
GOOD LUCK, SABRINA!
I JUST MIGHT MAKE IT BACK IN TIME AFTER ALL!
WOOO HOOO!

I HEAR CHEERING! THE GAME MUST STILL BE ON!
HUFF, HUFF
I CAN'T GO IN THERE WITH THIS BROOM! I BETTER HIDE IT FOR NOW!
JANITOR
TAK TAK TAK
HOME AWAY
I MADE IT!

THIS PLACE IS PACKED. WHERE AM I GOING TO SIT?
THERE'S AMY. WHY DOES SHE LOOK SO UPSET? OUR TEAM'S AHEAD BY SEVERAL POINTS!
WAIT A MINUTE... WHERE ARE ALL HER BLUE RIBBONS?
WAS SHE... LYING TO ME ABOUT BEING OFFERED ALL THOSE RIBBONS?
HOME
91
RUSH
HEY, AMY? WANT SOME POPCORN?
SURE, WHY NOT?

HOME
AWAY
93
91
LOOKS LIKE WE'RE GOING INTO OVERTIME!
TIME
00:05
HEH HEH
WHAP
HEY!
SPOKE TOO SOON, BRO!
00:03
TUM TUM
SWISH
YEAAAH!!
AND THE GROWLERS TAKE THE WIN WITH A SCORE OF 95-91! THIS YEAR THE BLUE RIBBON TROPHY BELONGS TO GREENDALE!
WOOO!
YEAH!
HA!
WE DID IT!
00:00
HOME
95

I'M SORRY I MISSED MOST OF THE TOURNAMENT, HARVEY.
THAT'S OKAY... YOU SHOWED UP AT THE END TO SEE US WIN. AND BESIDES...
...YES?
I KNOW IT SOUNDS STUPID BUT...
I WAS JUST GOING TO SAY THAT...
...THAT IT FELT LIKE YOU WERE THERE ANYWAY.
I KNOW WHAT YOU MEAN, HARVEY. IT'S NOT STUPID AT ALL. IN FACT...
IT'S KIND OF SWEET...

WHAT A NIGHT!
FSH
FSH

Chapter 3

COUNCILS AND CONCERTS
STORY AND ART
TANIA DEL RIO
INKS
JIM AMASH
COLORS
JASON JENSEN
LETTERS
JEFF POWELL
EDITOR
VICTOR GORELICK
EDITOR-IN-CHIEF
RICHARD GOLDWATER

SIGH...
OH WOW! "OBERON" IS HOLDING A CONCERT THIS WEEKEND! I THINK THAT'S ONE OF SABRINA'S FAVORITE GROUPS!
OBERON
SAT. 9:00 PM
SIGH...
IT SEEMS THAT LATELY I JUST CAN'T GET SABRINA OUT OF MY MIND!
NEWS
FFT
BUT WHAT'S THE USE? SHE OBVIOUSLY LIKES HARVEY MORE. SHE EVEN LEFT CLASS EARLY JUST TO BE WITH HIM!
THINGS MUST BE GETTING REALLY SERIOUS...
BUT I WON'T GIVE UP THAT EASILY! I KNOW... I'LL INVITE HER ON AN OFFICIAL DATE! THEN I'LL REALLY KNOW HOW SHE FEELS ABOUT ME! EVEN BETTER--I'LL TAKE HER TO THE OBERON CONCERT! YEAH! THERE'S NO WAY SHE'D TURN ME DOWN AFTER THAT!

WAIT UP, 'BRINA! I'LL "ZAP" TO THE MAGIC REALM WITH YOU. I'M ON MY WAY THERE FOR MY FIRST INTERVIEW WITH THE COUNCIL.
RUSTLE RUSTLE
THE COUNCIL? WHY WOULD YOU HAVE AN INTERVIEW WITH THEM?
WHAT? I'VE ONLY BEEN TALKING ABOUT IT ALL WEEK!
IT'S TRUE. BUT SABRINA'S ALWAYS TOO BUSY DAYDREAMING TO LISTEN!
WHAT? I DON'T REMEMBER YOU SAYING ANYTHING!
I WAS JUST TALKING ABOUT IT LAST NIGHT DURING DINNER!
I KNOW IT WILL BE DIFFICULT TO RUN FOR A PLACE ON COUNCIL, BUT I'D NEVER FORGIVE MYSELF IF I DIDN'T TRY!
GOOD FOR YOU, HILDA! I HOPE YOU MAKE IT! RIGHT, SABRINA?
HUH? YEAH, THE FOOD'S GREAT.
SEE WHAT I'M TALKING ABOUT?
COME TO MENTION IT... IT DOES SOUND A LITTLE FAMILIAR.
ALLOW ME TO REFRESH YOUR MEMORY. AS YOU KNOW, THE COUNCIL IS THE MATRIARCHAL GOVERNMENT IN THE MAGIC REALM, LED BY THE HIGH COUNCIL MEMBER, QUEEN SELES--
AUNT HILDA, I MAY NOT BE A GOOD LISTENER, BUT I'M NOT STUPID! OF COURSE I KNOW WHAT THE COUNCIL IS!

WELL, THAT'S A RELIEF! ANYWAY, ONE OF THE OLDEST COUNCIL MEMBERS HAS JUST RETIRED AND NOW THE COUNCIL IS LOOKING FOR SOMEONE TO TAKE HER PLACE.
THERE ARE A LOT OF PEOPLE WHO ARE APPLYING FOR THE POSITION, INCLUDING ME. I KNOW IT'S A LONG SHOT, BUT THE CHANCE DOESN'T COME AROUND VERY OFTEN. I JUST HAVE TO GIVE IT A SHOT!
WOW, HILDA! THAT'S SO COOL! I NEVER KNEW YOU HAD SUCH A DESIRE FOR POWER!
THAT'S NOT THE REASON!
RARRR
THEN WHY ARE YOU TRYING TO JOIN THE COUNCIL, HILDA? ISN'T THAT A LOT OF RESPONSIBILITY?
YES IT IS, SABRINA. THERE'S ONLY ROOM FOR SEVEN COUNCIL MEMBERS, BUT THEY INFLUENCE THE LIVES OF EVERYONE IN THE MAGIC REALM. I WANT TO MAKE A DIFFERENCE! I WANT TO MAKE THE MAGIC REALM A BETTER PLACE!
WOW, THIS IS A SIDE OF HILDA I'VE NEVER SEEN. I CAN'T BELIEVE SHE WANTS TO GO FOR SOMETHING SO BIG AND IMPORTANT!
IF ONLY I WAS MORE LIKE HER!

ALRIGHT HAVE FUN IN CLASS, SABRINA! WISH ME LUCK!
WOAH! WHAT'S THIS?
POOF
POOF
Ahem!
Miss Sabrina Spellman, you are hereby summoned to appear before the Czarina of Decree, Councilwoman Galiena in regards to recent events. Please hasten to the Council hall immediately.
WHY WOULD THE COUNCIL WANT TO SEE ME?!
MAYBE THEY WANT TO USE YOU AS A REFERENCE. AFTER ALL, THEY KNOW I'M APPLYING FOR THE EMPTY SEAT IN COUNCIL.
UGH, I HOPE THAT'S NOT THE REASON!
BUT I HAVE CLASS IN 10 MINUTES! I'LL BE LATE!
SABRINA, THIS IS THE COUNCIL WE'RE TALKING ABOUT! YOU HAVE TO GO! I'M SURE YOUR PROFESSOR WILL UNDERSTAND...
A VISIT TO THE COUNCIL IS NEVER GOOD... YOU MAY END UP A CAT LIKE ME!
PUT A LID ON IT, SALEM!!
POW

STATE YOUR BUSINESS!
I HAVE AN INTERVIEW WITH THE COUNCIL.
PROCEED!
I HAVE THIS LETTER...
AH, SABRINA SPELLMAN, I PRESUME? AND SALEM! IT'S BEEN A WHILE, HASN'T IT?
ENTIRELY TOO LONG.
I AM GALIENA, THE CZARINA OF DECREE. IT IS MY DUTY TO OVERSEE THE LAWS PLACED BY OUR COUNCIL AND ENSURE THAT OUR MAGICAL CITIZENS ARE NOT ABUSING THEIR POWERS IN ANY WAY.
WHY WOULD YOU WANT TO SPEAK TO SABRINA? SHE'S A GOOD KID!
HMPH. WELL, NOT ACCORDING TO OUR RECORDS.
NOW, WE USUALLY DON'T MEDDLE IN THE AFFAIRS OF THE MORTAL WORLD, BUT WE COULDN'T HELP BUT TAKE NOTICE WHEN SABRINA USED AND MISUSED ONE OF OUR 100 FORBIDDEN SPELLS--SPELLFREEZE!
BUT I DIDN'T EVEN CAST IT PROPERLY!
THAT IS BESIDE THE POINT. YOU ATTEMPTED TO CAST IT AND ENDANGERED OTHERS IN DOING SO. THERE'S MORE, HOWEVER.
GROAN

IT ALSO STATES IN OUR RECORDS THAT YOU HAVE RIDDEN A BROOM WITHOUT A LICENSE. YOU AREN'T THE ONLY TEENAGER TO BREAK THIS RULE, OF COURSE, BUT YOU MUST BE WARNED ALL THE SAME. IT IS ILLEGAL AND DANGEROUS TO OPERATE A BROOM WITHOUT A LICENSE!
MY PROFESSOR GAVE ME PERMISSION... BUT I COULD NEVER GET PROFESSOR LUNATA IN TROUBLE FOR HELPING ME OUT!
NOW, YOU'RE LUCKY WE AREN'T GOING TO DISCIPLINE YOU FOR YOUR ACTIONS. THIS IS MERELY A WARNING. TEENAGERS WILL DO FOOLISH THINGS AND WE UNDERSTAND THAT.
BUT YOU BETTER WATCH WHAT YOU DO FROM HERE ON OUT, BECAUSE WE'LL BE KEEPING AN EYE ON YOUR RECORD.
YES, MA'AM...
AND SALEM, YOU SHOULD KNOW BETTER! AFTER YOUR OWN PAST EXPERIENCES YOU THINK YOU WOULD TEACH SABRINA SOME BETTER JUDGMENT!
PERHAPS YOU CAN WORK ON BEING MORE OF A ROLE MODEL AND LESS OF AN ACCOMPLICE!
I'M JUST AN INNOCENT KITTY CAT!
MEW MEW
HILDA SPELLMAN, CORRECT? THE COUNCIL WILL SEE YOU IN THE MEETING ROOM IN 10 MINUTES FOR YOUR INTERVIEW.

SABRINA! I'M... SHOCKED! WHEN DID YOU RIDE A BROOM WITHOUT A LICENSE?
IT'S A LONG STORY. BESIDES, LIKE GALIENA SAID, IT'S NOT LIKE I'M THE FIRST KID TO BREAK THE RULES! WHY ARE THEY PICKING ON ME?
THAT'S NOT THE POINT! I EXPECT MORE FROM YOU, SABRINA! IT'S OBVIOUS THAT THEY'RE FOCUSING ON YOU BECAUSE I'M RUNNING FOR COUNCIL!
GREAT.
SABRINA, GETTING ON THE COUNCIL HAS ALWAYS BEEN A DREAM OF MINE.
IF YOU ARE GOING TO SUPPORT ME IN THIS, YOU HAVE TO BE MORE CAREFUL IN THE FUTURE. YOU'RE A SPELLMAN, SO YOUR ACTIONS WILL REFLECT ON ME WHETHER YOU LIKE IT OR NOT!
THAT'S NOT FAIR! SO, BASICALLY, IF YOU DON'T GET ON THE COUNCIL IT WILL ALL BE MY FAULT! GREAT.
I'M NOT GOING TO BLAME YOU, SABRINA. I'M JUST ASKING YOU TO SUPPORT ME. TO BE MORE CAREFUL ABOUT YOUR ACTIONS. PLEASE, IF YOU CAN'T DO IT FOR YOURSELF, DO IT FOR ME!
I'LL DO MY BEST, HILDA. I REALLY DO WANT YOU TO GET ON THE COUNCIL. I MEAN, IF THAT'S WHAT YOU REALLY WANT...
IT IS. THANK YOU, SABRINA. THIS MEANS A LOT TO ME.

SIGH...
MAN, EVERYONE'S GOING TO WONDER WHY I'M LATE FOR CLASS. THEY'LL ALL KNOW BY THE END OF THE NIGHT THAT I WAS REPRIMANDED BY THE COUNCIL.
AH, SABRINA. NICE OF YOU TO JOIN US.
WHISPER
GIGGLE
WHISPER
SABRINA, WHAT HAPPENED? IS EVERYTHING OKAY?
YOU DON'T WANT TO KNOW...
THE MOST IMPORTANT THING TO REMEMBER WITH ALCHEMY IS TO NOT MIX TWO CONFLICTING COMPONENTS...
WOW, SHE REALLY LOOKS UPSET. MAYBE SHE GOT IN A FIGHT WITH HARVEY!
THEN TONIGHT WILL BE THE PERFECT NIGHT TO ASK HER ON A DATE! THAT WILL CHEER HER UP FOR SURE.
AFTER CLASS...
OKONOMIYAKI
PANCAKE PIZZAS!
THE COUNCIL?!

THAT DOESN'T MAKE SENSE. WHY WOULD THE COUNCIL PICK ON YOU, SABRINA? THERE ARE TONS OF KIDS OUT THERE WHO HAVE DONE WORSE THINGS THAN YOU.
I GUESS IT'S BECAUSE MY AUNT HILDA IS RUNNING FOR COUNCIL.
I'D HATE TO HAVE A COUNCIL MEMBER AS A FAMILY MEMBER! I WOULDN'T BE ABLE TO DO ANYTHING!
I THINK THAT'S JUST WHAT YOU NEED, SHINJI.
FEH. I'VE HAD MY FAIR SHARE OF WARNINGS FROM THE COUNCIL AS IT IS.
REALLY? YOU HAVE?
YEAH! OF COURSE. "SHINJI, NO TELEPORTING INTO THE WARLOCK-WASTELANDS. SHINJI, NO MAGICAL PYROTECHNICS ALLOWED IN PUBLIC PARKS. SHINJI, NO USING ENCHANTED INK TO CHEAT ON STANDARDIZED TESTS."
WELL, AT LEAST I'M NOT THE ONLY ONE!
NO WONDER YOU'RE BUMMED, 'BRINA. I'D HATE TO HAVE THE MAGIC COUNCIL BREATHING DOWN MY NECK.
I JUST HAVE TO BE EXTRA CAREFUL FROM NOW ON...
CHEER UP, SABRINA. I HAVE JUST THE THING TO MAKE YOU FORGET ALL THIS COUNCIL BUSINESS.

SABRINA, I'D LIKE TO ASK YOU ON A DATE. "OBERON" IS THROWING A CONCERT THIS WEEKEND. I WANT YOU TO GO WITH ME AND HAVE A GOOD TIME.
SHINJI! I...
FORGET IT, SHINJI. SABRINA IS FOCUSING ON HARVEY RIGHT NOW. DON'T TRY TO GET IN-BETWEEN THEM.
NO, LLANDRA... IT'S OKAY. I THINK IT SOUNDS LIKE FUN, SHINJI. I'D BE HAPPY TO GO WITH YOU!
MEANWHILE, AT THE COUNCIL HALL...
QUEEN SELES! ATTENDANT TASSLE HERE WITH THE DAILY REPORT, YOUR MAJESTY.

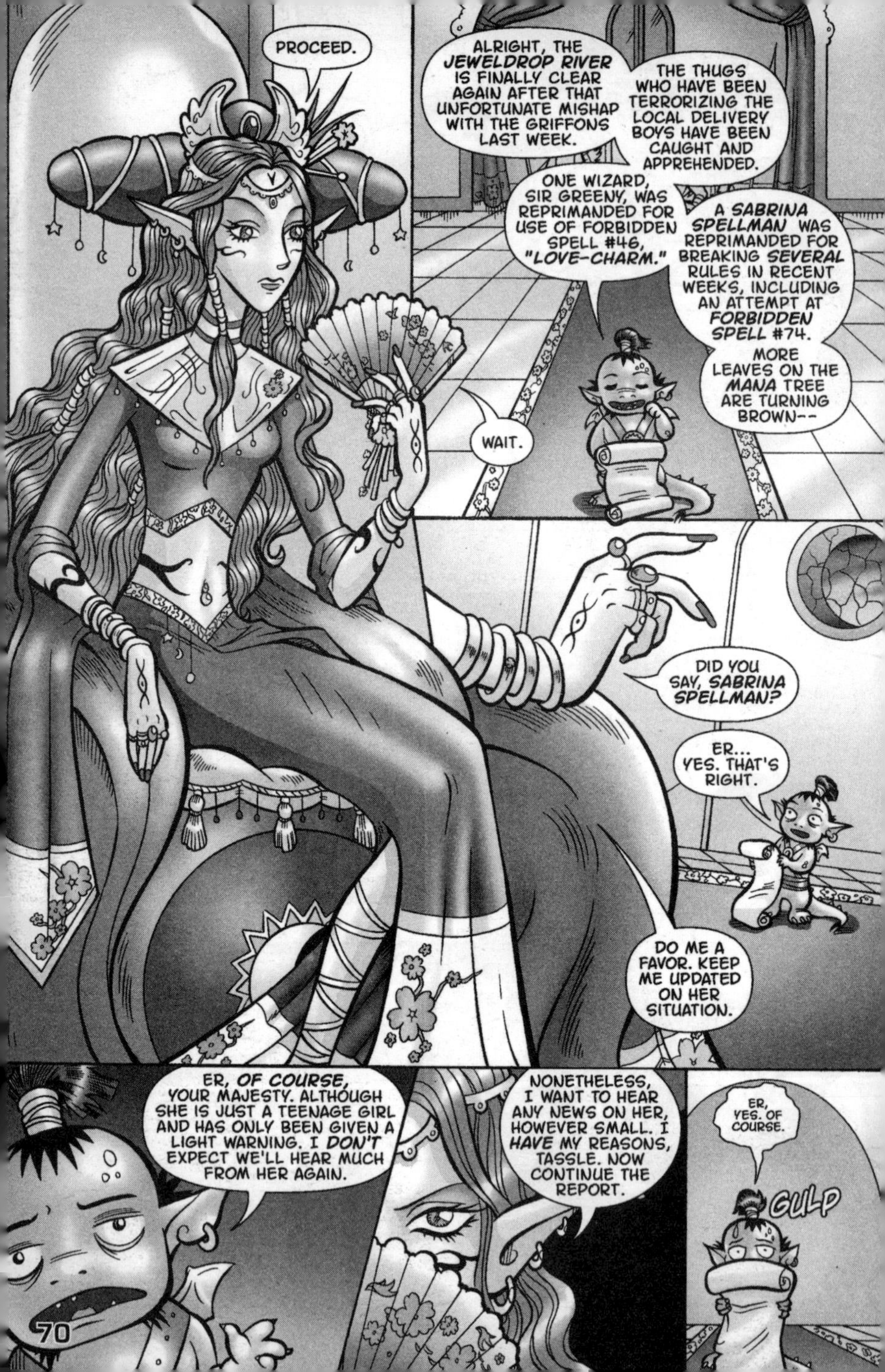
PROCEED.
ALRIGHT, THE JEWELDROP RIVER IS FINALLY CLEAR AGAIN AFTER THAT UNFORTUNATE MISHAP WITH THE GRIFFONS LAST WEEK.
THE THUGS WHO HAVE BEEN TERRORIZING THE LOCAL DELIVERY BOYS HAVE BEEN CAUGHT AND APPREHENDED.
ONE WIZARD, SIR GREENY, WAS REPRIMANDED FOR USE OF FORBIDDEN SPELL #46, "LOVE-CHARM."
A SABRINA SPELLMAN WAS REPRIMANDED FOR BREAKING SEVERAL RULES IN RECENT WEEKS, INCLUDING AN ATTEMPT AT FORBIDDEN SPELL #74.
MORE LEAVES ON THE MANA TREE ARE TURNING BROWN--
WAIT.
DID YOU SAY, SABRINA SPELLMAN?
ER... YES. THAT'S RIGHT.
DO ME A FAVOR. KEEP ME UPDATED ON HER SITUATION.
ER, OF COURSE, YOUR MAJESTY. ALTHOUGH SHE IS JUST A TEENAGE GIRL AND HAS ONLY BEEN GIVEN A LIGHT WARNING. I DON'T EXPECT WE'LL HEAR MUCH FROM HER AGAIN.
NONETHELESS, I WANT TO HEAR ANY NEWS ON HER, HOWEVER SMALL. I HAVE MY REASONS, TASSLE. NOW CONTINUE THE REPORT.
ER, YES. OF COURSE.
GULP

WHY DO I FEEL SO NERVOUS? I GUESS I JUST CAN'T BELIEVE SHINJI ASKED ME ON AN OFFICIAL DATE!
I'M EXCITED BUT...
I CAN'T HELP BUT FEEL A BIT GUILTY, TOO.
I CAN HARDLY BELIEVE IT, BUT YOU ACTUALLY LOOK NERVOUS, SHINJI!
I'M NOT NERVOUS, KEN. I NEVER GET NERVOUS ON DATES.
BUT I'D BE CRAZY TO TURN DOWN AN OBERON CONCERT!
AND WE ALL KNOW YOU'VE BEEN ON PLENTY OF THOSE!
YOU'RE JUST JEALOUS, KEN!
STILL, SHE MUST BE A PRETTY SPECIAL GIRL TO MAKE YOU SPEND THIS MUCH TIME GETTING READY!
SHE'S PRETTY COOL. SHE SHOULD BE HERE SOON.
BUT THIS PLACE IS A DUMP!
DING DONG
THAT'S HER! NO WORRIES, I GOT IT UNDER CONTROL.

SPARKLE
SPARKLE
ZAP
SPARKLE
HI, 'BRINA! COME ON IN!
WOW, SHINJI! NICE PLACE. IT'S A REAL BACHELOR PAD!
SABRINA, THIS IS MY BIG BRO KENICHI. KEN, THIS IS SABRINA.
HIS BROTHER?! HOW CAN THEY POSSIBLY BE RELATED?!
ALRIGHT, ARE YOU BOTH READY FOR ME TO ESCORT YOU TO THE CONCERT?
AW, KEN, WE CAN JUST TELEPORT OURSELVES.
HEH
SHINJI, YOU KNOW THERE ARE RULES ABOUT UNDERAGE TELEPORTATION TO SOCIAL EVENTS. WE DON'T WANT TO GET YOU TWO IN TROUBLE NOW.
HE'S RIGHT, SHINJI. I DON'T WANT TO GET IN TROUBLE!
FINE, FINE. LET'S GO.
TELE-ZAP

ALRIGHT KIDS, HAVE FUN! REMEMBER TO TAKE A MAGI-TAXI HOME SINCE I HAVE TO WORK THE NIGHT SHIFT TONIGHT.
RIGHT, KEN. WHATEVER YOU SAY.
TAXI
HE WORKS AT A SECURITY BOOTH IN THE MAGI-CITY. HE'S SUCH A STICKLER FOR RULES.
I CAN TELL THAT'S RUBBED OFF ON YOU.
ZAP
NOW, SABRINA, DON'T BE MAD BUT... I HAVEN'T ACTUALLY MANAGED TO GET TICKETS TO THE CONCERT YET.
WHAT?! SHINJI!
DON'T WORRY, IT WILL BE OKAY! WE'RE GONNA GET IN, OKAY?
HUH?
WELL... I'M SURE THERE'S SOMEONE AROUND HERE SELLING EXTRA TICKETS...
OKAY... READY... GET SET...
GO!
HEY!

SHINJI! WHAT DID YOU JUST DO?!
I FOUND AN OPENING AND WENT FOR IT. I GAVE US A LITTLE ZAP FOR A SPEED BOOST... JUST IN CASE.
ARE YOU CRAZY?! DO YOU KNOW HOW MUCH TROUBLE WE COULD GET INTO IF WE'RE CAUGHT? I'M SUPPOSED TO BE STAYING OUT OF TROUBLE, REMEMBER?
SHH, KEEP IT DOWN! NO ONE'S EVER GONNA NOTICE. AT LEAST NOT UNLESS YOU STOP YELLING SO LOUD!
SHINJI...
IT WILL BE OKAY. THERE'S TONS OF PEOPLE HERE. AND TRUST ME, NO ONE FROM THE COUNCIL WOULD COME WITHIN 10 MILES OF THIS CONCERT. I'M GONNA PROTECT YOU, OKAY?
HEY, EVERYONE! THANKS FOR COMING OUT TONIGHT! LET'S ALL HAVE A GOOD TIME!
NOW COME ON, LET'S FIND A GOOD SPOT. IT'S ABOUT TO START!
FIZZ
WHIR
POP
OOH!
WOW!

I'M TORN IN TWO
SO TORN!
YOU EACH LOOK AT ME
ASKING ME WITH YOUR EYES
I CAN'T DECIDE!
I JUST CAN'T HIDE!
I'M TORN IN TWO!

I NEVER THOUGHT
I'D BE CAUGHT UNDER YOUR SPELL
IT'S MORE THAN MAGIC, IT'S DESTINY
OH, I TRIED TO HOLD BACK
I TRIED NOT TO SEE
THAT YOU WERE THE ONE
THE ONLY ONE FOR ME.

THERE THEY ARE!

THAT WAS A WONDERFUL DATE, SHINJI. THANK YOU SO MUCH!
I HAD FUN TOO, SABRINA.
OHH, I GUESS WE SHOULD HAVE LEFT THE ARENA SOONER. ALL THE MAGI-TAXI'S HAVE BEEN TAKEN. NOW WE'LL HAVE TO WAIT A WHILE.
I HAVE A BETTER IDEA.
ZAP
SHINJI?
I KNOW A SPOT WITH AN AMAZING VIEW. IT WILL TAKE YOUR BREATH AWAY. I THOUGHT WE COULD SHARE A ROMANTIC BROOMSTICK RIDE TOGETHER...
OH, SHINJI... IT SOUNDS COOL BUT... WE STILL DON'T HAVE OUR LICENSES!
OH, IT WILL BE OKAY. THIS PLACE IS SO SECLUDED, NO ONE WILL EVER FIND OUT. BESIDES... I SAID I'D PROTECT YOU, RIGHT?

I WOULD GIVE ALMOST ANYTHING TO GO WITH SHINJI RIGHT NOW... BUT IT'S TOO RISKY. IF I GET CAUGHT AGAIN, I COULD RUIN HILDA'S CHANCES OF JOINING THE COUNCIL...
I... I'M SORRY, SHINJI. BUT I JUST CAN'T DO IT. I CAN'T RISK IT.
SABRINA! COME ON, LIVE A LITTLE! YOU'RE YOUNG AND FULL OF LIFE! LET'S TAKE ADVANTAGE OF THIS TIME BEFORE WE GET OLD AND BORING!
YOU DON'T UNDERSTAND, SHINJI! I DON'T WANT TO JEOPARDIZE MY AUNT!
YOU CAN'T HONESTLY BELIEVE THAT THE COUNCIL IS WATCHING YOUR EVERY MOVE? IF YOU DO, THEN YOU'RE FULL OF YOURSELF.
HEY! WHAT'S WITH THE PERSONAL ATTACK? YOU COULD BE A LITTLE MORE UNDERSTANDING, YOU KNOW!
I JUST THINK YOU'RE BEING PARANOID!
WHAT DO I DO? IF I TURN HIM DOWN NOW I COULD RUIN OUR CHANCES FOR A RELATIONSHIP. HE'LL THINK I'M SUCH A BABY! I DON'T WANT OUR FRIENDSHIP TO BREAK BECAUSE OF THIS! MAYBE I SHOULD JUST GO...
NO. I CAN'T DO IT. HILDA WOULD NEVER FORGIVE ME. I COULD NEVER FORGIVE ME!

COME ON, 'BRINA. YOU'RE OLD ENOUGH TO MAKE YOUR OWN DECISIONS. LET'S GO, OKAY? YOU WON'T REGRET IT.
SHINJI. I SAID NO. AND THAT IS MY OWN DECISION.
PLEASE, SABRINA! DON'T DO THIS. NOT AFTER WE HAD SUCH A GREAT TIME.
SHINJI! DROP IT! I DID HAVE A GREAT TIME, BUT YOU'RE RUINING IT JUST AS MUCH AS I AM RIGHT NOW. JUST TRY TO BE A LITTLE MORE UNDERSTANDING!
WHY DO YOU KEEP SAYING THAT? I AM UNDERSTANDING! I'M JUST NOT AS MUCH OF A WUSS AS HARVEY.
LEAVE HARVEY OUT OF THIS! AT LEAST HE WOULDN'T BE PUSHING ME TO BREAK THE RULES RIGHT NOW!
I GET IT. NOW I SEE THE REAL REASON YOU DON'T WANT TO GO WITH ME.
NO, SHINJI, IT'S NOT--
LLANDRA WAS RIGHT. I SHOULDN'T HAVE GOTTEN INVOLVED.
YOU JERK! ARE YOU JUST GONNA LEAVE ME HERE ALONE?!
SWOOSH

HOW CAN SHINJI BE SO NICE SOMETIMES AND SUCH AN INSENSITIVE JERK OTHER TIMES?
WHAT AM I GOING TO DO? IT DOESN'T LOOK LIKE THERE'S GOING TO BE ANYMORE MAGI-TAXIS. I CAN'T TELEPORT BY MYSELF... AND IT'S TOO LATE TO CALL ANYONE.
I GUESS I SHOULD CALL HILDA AND WAKE HER UP. SHE'LL BE SO MAD AT ME THOUGH...
AND SHE'LL ASK ME WHAT HAPPENED. I DON'T WANT TO TELL HER.
IF HILDA KNEW THAT SHINJI WAS PUSHING ME TO RIDE A BROOM ILLEGALLY, SHE WOULDN'T LET ME HANG OUT WITH HIM ANYMORE. BUT THEN, MAYBE SHINJI DOESN'T WANT TO HANG OUT WITH ME ANYWAY. I GUESS IT'S OVER...
AUNT HILDA? IT'S ME, SABRINA. CAN YOU...PICK ME UP?

DO YOU... WANT TO TALK ABOUT WHAT HAPPENED?
NOT REALLY.
I'M SORRY I WOKE YOU UP, HILDA. AND I'M SORRY YOU HAD TO COME GET ME.
THERE'S NO NEED TO APOLOGIZE. I'M HAPPY YOU CALLED ME. IT WAS THE RESPONSIBLE THING TO DO. IT WAS VERY ADULT OF YOU
SHE'S NOT MAD LIKE I THOUGHT SHE'D BE. MAYBE SHE UNDERSTANDS MORE THAN I THOUGHT SHE WOULD.
OH, AUNT HILDA. IT STARTED OFF SO GOOD. I WENT TO SHINJI'S HOUSE AND MET HIS BROTHER WHO'S A SECURITY GUARD. THEY'RE TOTAL OPPOSITES! HE ESCORTED US TO THE CONCERT EVEN THOUGH SHINJI WANTED US TO GO ALONE. THEN SHINJI ADMITTED HE DIDN'T HAVE TICKETS.
NO WAY!
I KNOW! I WAS SOOO UPSET! SO THEN, YOU WON'T BELIEVE WHAT HE DID. I KNOW YOU'RE GOING TO BE UPSET BUT HE...
I TOLD HILDA EVERYTHING. I STILL CAN'T BELIEVE SHE WASN'T FURIOUS WITH ME. SHE ACTUALLY SEEMED HAPPY THAT I WAS HONEST AND THAT I TALKED TO HER. ADULTS ARE SO WEIRD. MOST OF THE TIME IT FEELS LIKE THEY'RE AGAINST YOU, BUT EVERY NOW AND THEN YOU REALIZE THEY'RE ON YOUR SIDE...

I'M GLAD I TALKED TO HILDA. IT FEELS SO GOOD TO KNOW I CAN TRUST HER. BUT I STILL FEEL HORRIBLE ABOUT SHINJI. I BET HE HATES MY GUTS. HE PROBABLY THINKS I'M SUCH A BABY.
WHAT? IT'S 4 IN THE MORNING! WHO WOULD BE CALLING NOW?
CHIRP CHIRP
HELLO?
I'M SORRY FOR WAKING YOU.
I COULDN'T SLEEP.
ME NEITHER.
SABRINA... I WANTED TO SAY THAT I'M SORRY FOR EARLIER. I FEEL LIKE SUCH A CREEP. I SHOULDN'T HAVE PUSHED YOU LIKE THAT AND SAID THOSE MEAN THINGS.
OH, SHINJI! I THOUGHT YOU'D NEVER WANT TO TALK TO ME AGAIN!
AW, YOU THINK A LITTLE SPAT LIKE THAT WOULD STOP ME FROM TALKING TO MY FAVORITE GIRL? YOU KNOW I'LL ALWAYS BE YOUR FRIEND, EVEN WHEN WE DISAGREE...
THANKS, SHINJI... I FEEL SO MUCH BETTER NOW.
ME TOO.
BUT THAT CONCERT WAS AWESOME, WASN'T IT? I CAN'T STOP THINKING ABOUT THAT ONE PART IN THE LIGHTSHOW WHERE--
SABRINA! GO TO BED!
SORRY, SHINJI. I GOTTA GO. MY AUNT HAS TURNED INTO A GROWN-UP AGAIN.
GOOD NIGHT, 'BRINA.
GOOD NIGHT, SHINJI.
SIGH
END!

Chapter 4

THE MAGIC WITHIN
STORY + ART TANIA DEL RIO
INKS JIM AMASH
COLORS JASON JENSEN
LETTERS JEFF POWELL
EDITOR VICTOR GORELICK
EDITOR-IN-CHIEF RICHARD GOLDWATER

WHO: You! (Harvey) and one guest.
WHAT: Amy's Wicked Halloween Party
WHERE: Amy's house.
WHEN: 8:00 pm, Halloween night
WHY: Because there'll be a live dj, lots of food and refreshments, scary games and a fortune teller who does some pretty wild magic tricks! Be there... or are you too SCARED?
P.S. Costumes are required!
AW, COOL!
NOW I HAVE TO FIGURE OUT WHAT COSTUME TO WEAR. I DON'T REALLY LIKE DRESSING UP. WHAT ARE YOU GONNA BE?
I DON'T KNOW. I WASN'T INVITED
WHAT? ARE YOU SURE? DID YOU CHECK YOUR LOCKER?
YOU MIGHT STILL GET ONE...
YES, I DID. AND DON'T ACT SO SURPRISED. WE ALL KNOW THAT AMY LOVES TO EXCLUDE ME WHEREVER SHE CAN!
HEY, GUYS!
HEY, SHINJI!

SO WHAT DO YOU THINK? SHOULD I BE A ROGUISH PIRATE OR A USED-CAR SALESMAN?
HOW ABOUT AN OBNOXIOUS FLIRT WITH BLUE HAIR?
YOU GOT INVITED TOO, SHINJI?
OF COURSE! LET ME GUESS... AMY "FORGOT" YOUR INVITATION.
DON'T GO, YOU GUYS! HANG OUT WITH ME ON HALLOWEEN INSTEAD!
WAH
ER, I WOULD, NORMALLY... BUT, C'MON! IT'S GONNA BE A HUGE PARTY! YOU KNOW I CAN'T MISS OUT ON THAT!
NO ONE SAID YOU CAN'T COME TOO, SABRINA. MY INVITE SAYS I'M ALLOWED A GUEST. YOU CAN COME AS MINE IF YOU'D LIKE...
REALLY?! YOU'D LET ME COME AS YOUR DATE?
AS MY GUEST, YEAH!
DANG! WHY DIDN'T I THINK OF THAT?
THANKS, HARVEY. IT DOESN'T MATTER WHOSE PARTY IT IS. IF I'M GOING WITH YOU, I'LL HAVE A GOOD TIME!

NOW I HAVE TO FIGURE OUT WHAT I'M GOING TO BE!
HOW ABOUT AN INDECISIVE TEENAGE WITCH?
HA, HA! THAT WOULD BE CUTE!
WINTER
YEAH, AND YOU CAN GO AS A SLACKER WIZARD WHO CAN BARELY PASS POTIONS 1.
ON SECOND THOUGHT, MAYBE YOU SHOULD COME AS A GRUMPY OLD GHOUL.
AM I MISSING SOMETHING?
HIIIIIIII!
SPEAKING OF GHOULS.
HARVEY! SHINJI! DID YOU GUYS GET THE INVITATION I SENT YOU? IT'S GOING TO BE SUCH AN AWESOME PARTY!
MY OLDER COUSIN, D.J. DANNY C, WILL BE SPINNING RECORDS FOR US AND THIS NEW GIRL, GWENEVIVE, SHE IS SOOO COOL! I MET HER IN MATH CLASS. SHE'S TOTALLY INTO FORTUNE TELLING AND SHE KNOWS HOW TO DO THESE MAGIC SPELLS THAT ARE TOTALLY REAL!
IN FACT, SHE SAYS SHE'S AN ACTUAL WITCH! CAN YOU BELIEVE IT?! I THOUGHT SHE WAS CRAZY UNTIL I SAW SOME OF THE THINGS SHE CAN DO. UN-BE-LIEVABLE STUFF!
A WITCH!

YOU SAID HER NAME WAS GWENEVIVE?
YEAH! YOU MUST NOT BE VERY POPULAR IF YOU HAVEN'T EVEN HEARD OF HER YET! EVER SINCE GWEN MOVED TO GREENDALE, SHE'S TOTALLY BEEN THE TALK OF THE SCHOOL!
OF COURSE, YOU'RE JUST A LITTLE SOPHOMORE. WHAT WOULD YOU KNOW ABOUT A POPULAR NEW JUNIOR?
WINTER DANCE
WELL, SEE YOU AT THE PARTY, GUYS! AND IF YOU HAVE ANY CUTE FRIENDS, BRING THEM ALONG TOO!
THAT GIRL REALLY DOESN'T LIKE ME!
DON'T LET HER GET TO YOU, SABRINA. BESIDES, SHE SAID WE COULD BRING ANY CUTE FRIENDS WE HAD, RIGHT?
AWW..
I KNOW HARVEY'S RIGHT. I REALLY SHOULDN'T LET AMY GET TO ME LIKE THAT. BUT I CAN'T HELP IT! SHE'S ALWAYS TRYING TO CAUSE TROUBLE!
AND WHO IS SHE CALLING UNPOPULAR? WHY WOULD I KNOW ANYTHING ABOUT SOME NEW GIRL, ANYWAY? IT'S NOT LIKE I HAVE THAT MANY CLASSES WITH JUNIORS!
AND WHAT'S ALL THIS ABOUT THAT WITCH, GWENEVIVE, ANYWAY?! WHO DOES SHE THINK SHE IS, USING HER POWERS LIKE THAT IN THE MORTAL REALM?!

OOF
I'm Bored.
1:00pm
x+y=-2
ax2 + 3b = ?
OWW...
WOW...
The only friend I have right now
is the magic within me
it fills me up with wonder
its source a mystery
Dare I dream that it somehow
might come from within me?
or is it an illusion
and will it one day flee?
Let me keep it for a while
and let the others see
for if they like my magic
then maybe they'll like me.
SORRY, I--
GIVE THAT BACK! WATCH WHERE YOU'RE GOING, NEXT TIME!
SNATCH
HEY! YOU COULD LOOK, TOO, YOU KNOW!
WHATEVER. I'M LATE FOR CLASS AS IT IS. MOVE IT!
NOT UNTIL YOU APOLOGIZE!
GWENEVIVE
GWENEVIVE!

SO *YOU'RE* THIS SO-CALLED WITCH!
WHAT'S IT TO *YOU?* LOOK, I DON'T HAVE TIME FOR THIS.
GRAB
HEY!
WAIT! WHO DO YOU THINK YOU ARE USING YOUR POWERS IN THE *MORTAL* REALM FOR EVERYONE TO SEE? WHY AREN'T YOU GOING TO SCHOOL IN THE *MAGIC* REALM, LIKE *MOST* WITCHES?
WHAT? WHAT ARE YOU TALKING ABOUT? YOU'RE *CRAZY!* LET ME GO!
SHE *DOESN'T* KNOW!
YOU-- YOU'RE A FAKE! A *WANNABE!*
HOW *DARE* YOU?! MY POWERS ARE *VERY* REAL! ANYWAY, I DON'T HAVE TO PROVE *ANYTHING* TO *YOU!*
NOW I SEE WHY SHE AND AMY MUST GET ALONG SO WELL.

HE NEXT DAY
I DON'T KNOW, SALEM. I CAN'T FIND A COSTUME I LIKE! MAYBE I'LL JUST GO AS A WITCH AGAIN.
YOU GO AS A WITCH EVERY YEAR!
WELL, LET'S KEEP LOOKING. THERE'S A COUPLE MORE STORES DOWN THE STREET I WANT TO TRY.
JINGLE
OH, GREAT!
WHAT?
IT'S GWENEVIVE
SHE'S THAT WANNABE WITCH THAT WAS SO MEAN TO ME! LET'S STAY HERE UNTIL SHE LEAVES.
YEAH, I DON'T LIKE THE LOOK OF... THAT...
DOG...
GLARE

ON SECOND THOUGHT, LET'S GET OUT OF HERE. THAT DOG-- I'VE SEEN ITS EYES BEFORE! IT'S NOT A NORMAL DOG!
THAT LITTLE THING? DON'T BE SILLY! BESIDES, I'M NOT DONE SHOPPING YET. BUT DON'T WORRY, SALEM, I WON'T WET THE WIDDLE PUPPY HURT YOU!
HOUSE OF TAROT
IT'S ALONE! SABRINA, I'M TELLING YOU, THAT DOG IS PURE EVIL! IF YOU DON'T WANT TO LEAVE, THEN LET'S AT LEAST CONFRONT IT TOGETHER!
UHH... OKAY.
HI, PUPPY WUPPY! YOUR NAME IS PUMPKIN, YES IT IS! THAT'S WHAT YOUR WIDDLE TAGGY WAGGY SAYS! OOOH! YOU RE SUCH A WIDDLE CUTIE!
ARE WE DONE "CONFRONTING" IT, YET?
NO... IT'S HIDING SOMETHING!
FINE. THEN YOU CAN CONTINUE THE INTERROGATION! I'VE GOT MORE SHOPPING TO DO!
ACK

BOO!
WAAH!!
I KNEW IT! I KNEW YOU WEREN'T JUST A REGULAR DOG!
C-CORWYN! I CAN'T BELIEVE IT!
WELL I SUPPOSE I SHOULD BE FLATTERED THAT YOU REMEMBER ME!
YES, IT IS I! HUNDREDS OF YEARS AGO YOU AND I WERE ENSNARED IN A BITTER RIVALRY OVER WHO WOULD TAKE OVER THE MAGIC REALM FIRST! OH, THOSE WERE THE DAYS! OUR ARMIES WERE AMASSED, OUR SPELLS AT THE READY! WE WERE EACH SO CLOSE TO OUR GOALS!
BUT I WAS CAUGHT BY THE MAGIC COUNCIL AND TURNED INTO A CAT! AND YOU! WELL IT SEEMS THEY CAUGHT YOU AS WELL. OTHERWISE, YOU WOULD STILL BE A POWERFUL SORCERESS AND NOT A DUMPY LITTLE DOG!

HALLOWEEN NIGHT
SO I SEE YOU DECIDED TO BE A WITCH AGAIN! YOUR BLACK CAT IS A GOOD PROP, TOO!
WHAT CAN I SAY? IT SUITS ME!
WHO ARE YOU CALLING A "PROP"?
HERE WE ARE!
PARTY!
I'LL BE RIGHT BACK, 'BRINA. I'M GONNA GO SAY HI TO SOME OF THE GUYS FROM MY TEAM.
THERE'S SHINJI! I'LL GO SAY HELLO.
HEY, SHINJI!
SABRINA! SO YOU DECIDED TO COME, AFTER ALL! MEET MY DATE, THE LOVELY BELLE OF THE MASQUERADE BALL!
HE BROUGHT A DATE! SHE LOOKS BEAUTIFUL! BUT IF SHINJI WAS GOING TO BRING SOMEONE, WHY DIDN'T HE ASK ME?

HEY 'BRINA. YOU SEEMED INTERESTED IN THAT GWEN GIRL AMY TOLD US ABOUT. SHE'S OVER THERE DOING FORTUNE TELLING AND MAGIC TRICKS IF YOU WANNA GO SEE.
I THINK I'VE LOST INTEREST.
COME ON, 'BRINA. LET'S SEE WHAT THIS GWEN IS ALL ABOUT.
IT LOOKS REAL, HUH?
I THOUGHT YOU SAID SHE WAS A FAKE!
THAT'S WHAT I THOUGHT! SHE DIDN'T SEEM TO KNOW ANYTHING ABOUT THE MAGIC REALM!
THERE'S NO DOUBT ABOUT IT, THOUGH. THAT'S REAL MAGIC!
TA-DA!
...WHO~?
IT'S A WIG!
HA HA! DON'T WORRY, SABRINA. IT'S JUST LLANDRA! WE CAN TRUST HER!
HEE
HEE
THAT'S WHAT I USED TO THINK.
SO! LOOK WHO DECIDED TO CRASH MY PARTY!

I DIDN'T EXPECT TO SEE YOU HERE, SABRINA!
SHE'S MY GUEST!
GLOAT
HARVEY... I'M DISAPPOINTED!
WHAT AN ACTRESS!
AMY! WAIT!
PSST, SABRINA!
SABRINA, I THINK I'VE FIGURED OUT HOW GWENEVIVE IS ABLE TO USE MAGIC!
HOW?
HER DOG!
PUMPKIN?
NO! CORWYN!
I TOLD YOU THAT GWENEVIVE'S DOG WAS ACTUALLY A SORCERESS I USED TO KNOW NAMED CORWYN. SHE WAS SUPER POWERFUL!
THAT MAY BE TRUE, SALEM. BUT SHE SHOULD HAVE LOST ALL HER MAGICAL ABILITY WHEN SHE WAS TURNED INTO AN ANIMAL, JUST LIKE YOU.
JUST WATCH!

THE DOG... IT'S LIKE... IT'S A PUPPET MASTER!
EVERY MOVE THE DOG MAKES IS MIMICKED BY GWENEVIVE. I DOUBT SHE EVEN REALIZES THAT HER "MAGIC" IS BEING CHANNELED THROUGH HER BY THAT DOG!
CREEEEEPY!
I TOLD YOU THAT WASN'T JUST ANY AVERAGE DOG! IT'S CORWYN AND IT'S SERIOUS BUSINESS IF SHE IS STILL ABLE TO USE MAGIC IN HER DOG FORM!
WAIT A MINUTE...

IF GWEN'S MAGIC IS COMING FROM THE DOG... THEN IF WE REMOVE THE DOG... SHE'LL HAVE NO MORE MAGIC!
SABRINA! I DIDN'T KNOW YOU HAD IT IN YOU!
I DON'T! THAT'S WHY YOU'RE GOING TO HELP ME!
SABRINA, AREN'T YOU BEING A LITTLE CHILDISH? THE POOR GIRL DOESN'T EVEN REALIZE THAT THAT MAGIC ISN'T HER OWN!
POOR GIRL? YOU DON'T EVEN KNOW WHO SHE IS! SHE WAS A TOTAL JERK TO ME THE OTHER DAY!
IT COULD HAVE BEEN A MISUNDERSTANDING. MAYBE YOU SHOULD JUST TALK TO HER...
SABRINA, I KNOW WHAT YOU'RE THINKING. YOU DON'T WANT TO MESS WITH CORWYN. TRUST ME, I KNOW!
SHINJI! YOU KNOW WHAT TO DO!
SURE THING, SABS! SIT BACK, RELAX AND ENJOY THE SHOW!
HEY, POOCHIE!
SWIPE
YIP!

LET'S SEE HOW YOU CAN USE MAGIC NOW, GWEN!
THIS IS STUPID!
YEOWCH!!
CHOMP
IT...IT'S NOT WORKING! I CAN'T DO IT! MY MAGIC!
IT'S GONE!
HEY, GWEN! WHAT HAPPENED? I WANTED TO SEE YOU DO THAT SPELL WITH THE FLOATING SPARKLY THINGS!
SURE! JUST, JUST A SECOND!
I GUESS YOU'RE NOT A REAL WITCH AFTER ALL! I ALMOST FELL FOR IT, TOO!
WHAT A BUNCH OF SUCKERS WE WERE!
BUT I AM A REAL WITCH! JUST GIVE ME A SECOND-- I'LL GET MY POWERS BACK!
TOO BAD. I ALMOST WISH IT WAS REAL. THAT WOULD HAVE BEEN SO COOL...
LAME. SHE SHOULD JUST GIVE IT UP BY NOW.
BUT IT IS REAL!
IT... WAS.

SO, SABRINA. DO YOU FEEL BETTER NOW?
...NO.
I'M GOING TO GO FIND SHINJI. I GOTTA GET THAT DOG BACK.
THERE YOU ARE!
OH, THANK GOODNESS! I DON'T THINK I COULD HANDLE THIS DOG MUCH LONGER!
ALRIGHT, 'BRINA. SEE YOU AROUND. I'M GONNA GET BACK TO THE PARTY!
RRRRRRR
SABRINA... I WOULD PUT CORWYN DOWN NOW. I DON'T THINK SHE LIKES BEING HELD LIKE THAT.
RRRRRRR
I'M JUST TRYING TO FIGURE OUT HOW SHE CAN STILL USE MAGIC WHILE IN THE FORM OF A DOG. DOES THAT MEAN YOU MIGHT BE ABLE TO USE MAGIC TOO, SALEM?
YOU FOOL! THAT HAIRBALL WILL NEVER REGAIN HIS POWERS! AS FOR ME, WELL...
ZAP
GASP

SIGH...
I KNEW MY MAGIC WOULDN'T LAST FOREVER... I JUST WISH IT LASTED A LITTLE WHILE LONGER... EVERYONE MUST THINK I'M SUCH A FRAUD.
OH, MY STARS! SALEM! WHAT IS GOING ON?!
HUH?
GASP!
HA HA HA!
CORWYN!
WHINE WHINE

HOW DID YOU LEAVE YOUR DOG FORM? THE MAGIC COUNCIL SHOULD HAVE MADE IT IMPOSSIBLE!
MY HIDING PLACE HAS GROWN OLD. IT'S TIME FOR ANOTHER!
HA! I WAS NEVER FOOLISH ENOUGH TO BE CAUGHT BY THE COUNCIL LIKE YOU WERE!
WHAT? BUT THEN WHY--
YOU SEEM TO HAVE FORGOTTEN THAT I AM A MASTER SHAPE-TAKER! WHEN THE COUNCIL PUT ME ON THEIR MOST-WANTED LIST, I FLED TO THE MORTAL REALM AND TOOK OVER THE FORM OF MANY THINGS, THIS PITIFUL DOG INCLUDED! AND SO I HAVE SURVIVED FOR CENTURIES!
AND FOR WHAT? YOU BASICALLY IMPRISONED YOURSELF! THE COUNCIL WOULD THANK YOU!
I MAY HAVE IMPRISONED MYSELF, BUT I ALWAYS HELD THE KEY! MY MAGIC! AND WHILE MY POWERS ARE WEAKER IN THIS MORTAL WORLD, WHAT BETTER WAY TO STRENGTHEN MY SKILLS THAN TO PRACTICE THROUGH A GULLIBLE GIRL WHO WANTS SO BADLY TO BE A WITCH! HA! PATHETIC!
WHAT A WASTE OF YOUR TIME! THE MAGIC COUNCIL WILL BE HAPPY TO KNOW YOU'RE STILL AROUND-- AND WEAKER AS WELL!
NO! I HAVE WORKED TOO HARD TO BE CAUGHT BY SOME TEENAGE WITCH!

SHE'S GETTING AWAY!
SALEM! STAY WITH PUMPKIN! I'M GOING AFTER HER!
WHAT AM I GOING TO DO? IF I USE MAGIC TO TRY AND CATCH CORWYN, PEOPLE MIGHT SEE! MAYBE THE COUNCIL WOULD FORGIVE ME FOR A CASE LIKE THIS. BUT AM I EVEN STRONG ENOUGH? I DON'T KNOW!
WICKED COSTUME!
WOAH!
IS THIS ANOTHER PART OF YOUR HALLOWEEN EXTRAVAGANZA?
...

THERE ARE TOO MANY PEOPLE! I DON'T HAVE THE STRENGTH TO TELE-ZAP! WHERE IS THE EXIT? I MUST BUY SOME TIME WITH THE...
...LIGHTS OUT!
EEEEEEK!!
THE LIGHTS!!!
WAH HA HA!
OW!
THAT WAS SCARY!
HA HA HA!
IS THIS A MURDER-MYSTERY GAME?
SHE'S GONE!
DID I LOSE HER? WAIT!
IF CORWYN COULD TAKE THE SHAPE OF THAT DOG THEN... SHE CAN TAKE THE SHAPE OF ANYTHING IN THIS ROOM!

AH-HA!
I MIGHT NOT HAVE THE SKILL TO TRAP A FULL-GROWN SORCERESS, BUT I DO HAVE THE POWER TO TRAP A PUMPKIN!
ZAP-BIND
MMPH! MMPH!
I'VE GOT TO GET THIS TO THE MAGIC COUNCIL ASAP! I'LL TELE-ZAP FROM THE BACKYARD. NO ONE WILL SEE ME THERE.
HEY, SABRINA! THERE YOU ARE! I WAS--
SORRY, HARV! I GOTTA GET GOING! THANKS FOR A GREAT NIGHT!
BUT YOU'RE RUNNING TOWARDS THE BACKYARD! AND... WHY ARE YOU TAKING ONE OF AMY'S JACK-O-LANTERNS?!
...

JUST GOT TO MAKE SURE NO ONE WILL SEE ME...
SNIFF SNIFF
HUH?
IT'S GWEN! LUCKILY, SHE DOESN'T SEE ME. IF I TELE-ZAP QUICKLY, SHE WON'T EVEN NOTICE!
I REALLY SHOULD JUST GO...
UM... GWENEVIVE?
I KNOW THE FIRST TIME WE, UH, RAN INTO EACH OTHER, WE DIDN'T EXACTLY GET OFF ON THE RIGHT FOOT. BUT I WANTED TO APOLOGIZE BECAUSE WHATEVER YOU'RE FEELING RIGHT NOW... IT'S ALL BECAUSE OF ME. I'M SORRY.
I KNEW THE MAGIC WASN'T MY OWN. SOMEHOW I KNEW IT WOULDN'T LAST.
EVEN SO, I HAD WISHED FOR IT FOR SO LONG... SOMETHING MAGICAL, SOMETHING UNIQUE. WHEN THE FIRST SPARKS CAME FROM MY FINGERS... IT WAS LIKE A GIFT. I KNEW IT WASN'T MY OWN, BUT I STILL FOOLED MYSELF INTO THINKING IT MIGHT HAVE COME FROM WITHIN ME.

LOOK, I KNOW YOU GOT UPSET WHEN YOU SAW ME READING YOUR POETRY. BUT IT WAS REALLY GOOD. YOU HAVE A GIFT. THAT'S MAGIC IN ITS OWN WAY.
I DIDN'T MEAN TO BE SO RUDE. I WAS IN A BAD MOOD AND I TOOK IT OUT ON YOU. THEN, WHEN YOU READ MY POEM, I GOT EVEN MORE UPSET BECAUSE I FELT EMBARRASSED.
BUT IT WAS WONDERFUL! I ONLY WISH I COULD WRITE LIKE THAT! I WOULD GIVE ANYTHING TO HAVE A TALENT! I DON'T HAVE A SINGLE THING THAT I'M REALLY GOOD AT.
BUT... YOU CAN USE MAGIC!
HOW... WHERE DID YOU GET THAT IDEA?
I SAW WHAT HAPPENED BETWEEN YOU AND THAT... THAT WOMAN. I SAW THE MAGIC YOU USED TO TRY AND STOP HER.
OH, AND YOUR CAT FILLED ME IN ON THE REST.
YOU DON'T SEEM VERY SURPRISED BY ALL THIS!
I ALREADY BELIEVED IN MAGIC BEFORE ALL THIS HAPPENED. I COULD ALWAYS FEEL ITS PRESENCE AROUND ME, EBBING AND FLOWING. NOW, IT'S LIKE MY EYES HAVE BEEN OPENED. I CAN SEE MAGIC FOR WHAT IT IS, BUT I CAN NO LONGER TOUCH IT. BUT... I'M STILL HAPPY TO KNOW THAT IT REALLY DOES EXIST. I HAVE THAT, AT LEAST.
SHE EVEN TALKS POETIC!

GWEN... CAN I TRUST YOU TO KEEP THIS TO YOURSELF? MORTALS AREN'T SUPPOSED TO KNOW ABOUT MAGIC. IF THE MAGIC COUNCIL FOUND OUT HOW MUCH YOU KNOW, THEY WOULD TRY TO HAVE YOUR MEMORIES WIPED!
IT'S A SECRET I'VE KEPT ALL MY LIFE. I ONLY TRIED SHARING IT WITH PEOPLE WHEN I FOUND OUT THAT I COULD USE IT.
THAT WAS A MISTAKE. I THOUGHT IT WOULD GET PEOPLE TO LIKE ME MORE. IT JUST GOES TO SHOW THAT IF PEOPLE DON'T BELIEVE IN SOMETHING TO BEGIN WITH, THEY MOST LIKELY NEVER WILL. EVEN IF IT'S RIGHT BEFORE THEIR EYES.
I DON'T KNOW HER VERY WELL BUT, SOMEHOW, I THINK I CAN TRUST HER.
THERE YOU ARE, SABRINA! PUMPKIN FINALLY *WOKE* UP. ALTHOUGH, SHE SEEMS TO HAVE GOTTEN A STRANGE *SIDE-EFFECT* FROM HAVING CORWYN TAKE HER OVER FOR SO LONG.
HI!
YOU *TALK!*
YEAH! ISN'T IT GREAT? I CAN NOW TELL YOU EVERYTHING THAT IVE HAD ON MY MIND FOR SOOOOOO LONG! FIRST OF ALL, I CAN'T STAND THAT DRY KIBBLE YOU FEED ME! HOW COME I DON'T GET SOME REAL FOOD ONCE IN A WHILE? ALSO WHY CAN'T I CHASE SQUIRRELS? IT'S MY FAVORITE THING! OH, AND ALSO...
IT SEEMS SOME MAGICAL *"RESIDUE"* WAS LEFT BEHIND! IT SEEMS SHE'S GOING TO BE A BIT OF A CHATTERBOX... JUST BECAUSE SHE CAN BE!

HE MAGIC COUNCIL
I MUST SAY, MISS SPELLMAN, I'M QUITE IMPRESSED!
CZARINA OF CREATION
SHIMAR CZARINA OF TREASURY
GALIENA CZARINA OF DECREE
QUEEN SELES CZARINA OF BALANCE
BERNADETTE CZARINA OF CHARITY
LIBRA CZARINA OF KNOWLEDGE
IGNACIA CZARINA OF DEFENSE
TH-THANK YOU!
I WILL ENJOY GIVING CORWYN THE SENTENCE SHE HAS DESERVED FOR SO MANY YEARS!
IT MUST HAVE BEEN FRIGHTENING STANDING BEFORE SUCH A POWERFUL SORCERESS! BUT YOU COMPOSED YOURSELF WELL!
YES, BINDING HER IN THIS PUMPKIN WAS QUITE A RESOURCEFUL MOVE!
MISS SPELLMAN...
GIVE YOUR AUNT HILDA MY PERSONAL REGARDS. IT SEEMS WE ARE NEARING A DECISION ON WHO WILL FILL THE SEVENTH SEAT ON THIS COUNCIL!

RING RING
HELLO?
SAAAAALEM! IT'S FOR YOOOOOU! IT'S A GIIIRL!
STOMP STOMP
GRUMBLE GRUMBLE
...HI, PUMPKIN. DIDN'T YOU JUST CALL ME TWO HOURS AGO? ...WHAT? NO...I DIDN'T SEE THAT SHOW ON TV... YOU WANT TO TELL ME ALL ABOUT IT? ...SURE, I HAVE HALF-AN-HOUR TO SPARE...
IT LOOKS LIKE SALEM HAS MADE A TALKATIVE NEW FRIEND!
WHETHER HE LIKES IT OR NOT!
GIGGLE GIGGLE
END!!

Chapter 5

Winter Wallflower
Writer & Artist Tania Del Rio Inker Jim Amash
Colorist Jason Jensen Letterer Jeff Powell
Victor Gorelick
Editor
Richard Goldwater
Editor-In-Chief
Orange Kiss

AHH! THE FIRST SNOW OF THE YEAR! IT'S ABOUT TIME, TOO!
UGH, I HATE SNOW!
YOU HATE EVERYTHING.
AND YOU THINK EVERYTHING IS SOOOO CUTE AND WONDERFUL!
NYAH
NYAH
I KNOW! I'LL HOLD A WINTER SLUMBER PARTY! THERE'S NOTHING LIKE HANGING OUT WITH FRIENDS IN A WARM HOUSE WITH HOT COCOA AND CHICK FLICKS.
RANDOM THOUGHT
SOUNDS GIRLY. I'LL BE HIBERNATING...
I'LL INVITE LLANDRA OF COURSE. MAYBE I'LL EVEN INVITE GWENEVIVE. THE MORE THE MERRIER, RIGHT?

SABRINA... NEED I REMIND YOU THAT EVERY TIME YOU HAVE A SLEEPOVER WITH LLANDRA YOU TWO END UP IN A BIG FIGHT?
WE DO?
SQUABBLE
ANOTHER TIME LLANDRA WAS UPSET BECAUSE YOU DIDN'T LIKE THE WAY SHE STYLED YOUR HAIR, ANOTHER TIME--
WAAH!
LAST TIME YOU TWO GOT IN A FIGHT OVER THE RULES OF TRUTH OR DARE.
OKAY, OKAY. I GET THE IDEA.
BUT I DOUBT WE'LL FIGHT THIS TIME--I'M IN TOO GOOD OF A MOOD LATELY TO GET UPSET OVER PETTY THINGS!
IT'S TRUE... YOU HAVE BEEN IN A GOOD MOOD LATELY. WHAT'S UP?
VERY SUSPICIOUS...
CAN'T I BE IN A GOOD MOOD JUST FOR THE SAKE OF IT?
OKAY, FINE. THE TRUTH IS, I'M REALLY EXCITED ABOUT THE GREENDALE WINTER DANCE THAT'S COMING UP. NOW THAT I'M A SOPHOMORE, I CAN GO!
YAY!
A DANCE, HUH? SOUNDS LIKE TROUBLE.

SEVERAL NIGHTS LATER...
DING DONG
THANKS FOR COMING, GUYS--WE'RE GONNA HAVE FUN!
IT'S BEEN FOREVER SINCE WE LAST DID THIS!
I'VE NEVER BEEN TO A SLUMBER PARTY BEFORE...
REALLY?! YOU POOR THING!
HUH?!
LATER...
SO LET ME GET THIS STRAIGHT... YOU'RE BOTH WITCHES?!
YEAH! SHINJI IS TOO. WELL, A WIZARD. THAT'S A MALE WITCH.
HOW MANY OF YOU ARE THERE?!
QUITE A FEW. MOST OF US LIVE IN THE MAGIC REALM, THOUGH. SOME, LIKE ME AND MY AUNTS, LIKE TO LIVE IN THE MORTAL REALM. BUT WE STILL GO BACK AND FORTH A LOT.
MAGIC REALM?!
SABRINA...
YEAH, IT'S A WHOLE OTHER WORLD THAT'S PURELY MAGICAL. THERE'S A MANA TREE THAT PROVIDES ALL THE MAGICAL ENERGY. ALSO, THE REALM'S RULED BY THE 7 MEMBERS OF THE MAGIC COUNCIL, INCLUDING THE ELVEN QUEEN, SELES. SHE'S SOOOO PRETTY!
AN ELF!! THIS IS ALL TOO MUCH TO TAKE IN!
YEAH, THERE ARE TONS OF ELVES. AND MINOTAURS AND SATYRS AND UNICORN-PEOPLE AND WEREWOLVES AND FAERIES. AND HUMANS LIKE ME AND LLANDRA, OF COURSE, AND A BUNCH OF OTHER KINDS OF MAGICAL CREATURES.

IT'S JUST SO AMAZING... I CAN'T BELIEVE THERE'S THIS WHOLE OTHER SECRET WORLD!
"SECRET" BEING THE KEY WORD, THERE.
CAN MORTALS GO THERE? YOU KNOW, JUST TO VISIT?
I'M ACTUALLY NOT SURE.
WE WENT OVER THIS IN MAGICAL HISTORY CLASS! MORTALS HAVE BROKEN INTO THE MAGIC REALM BEFORE AND IT'S ALWAYS HAD DISASTROUS RESULTS. THAT'S WHY WE KEEP THE MAGIC WORLD SECRET FROM MORTALS!
YEAH, BUT GWEN DOESN'T COUNT. SHE'S NOT LOOKING FOR TROUBLE LIKE THOSE OTHER MORTALS WERE. SHE'S OUR FRIEND.
YEAH, I'M NOT GOING TO TELL ANYONE ELSE! I SWEAR!
OH, GWENEVIVE. YOUR MOTHER'S ON THE PHONE DOWNSTAIRS.
OH, OKAY, THANKS!

CLICK
WHAT ON EARTH ARE YOU DOING?!
WHAT?
WHY ARE YOU TELLING GWEN ALL THESE THINGS? IT'S BAD ENOUGH THAT SHE LEARNED YOU WERE A WITCH AT AMY'S HALLOWEEN PARTY! IF THE COUNCIL EVER FOUND OUT, THEY'D HAVE HER MEMORIES WIPED!
I KNOW! IT'S JUST... I FEEL LIKE I CAN TRUST HER.
IF YOU CARE ABOUT GWEN THEN YOU SHOULD PROTECT HER BY NOT TELLING HER ANYTHING! DO YOU KNOW WHICH COUNCIL MEMBER WOULD BE RESPONSIBLE FOR ERASING HER MEMORY IF SHE WAS DISCOVERED?
THE... CZARINA OF MEDIATION?
AND WHICH POSITION IS HILDA CURRENTLY SEEKING?
THE... CZARINA OF MEDIATION.

HEY, GUYS! SO, I JUST HAVE A FEW MORE QUESTIONS ABOUT THE MAGIC REALM...
BOYS!
ACTUALLY, LET'S TALK ABOUT SOMETHING ELSE FOR A WHILE.
OKAY, GWEN. YOU'RE NEW SO YOU HAVE TO ANSWER FIRST. WHO DO YOU LIKE?
OHHH, DON'T MAKE ME ANSWER!
COME ON, GWEN! FESS UP!
OH, THIS IS SO EMBARRASSING! YOU GUYS HAVE TO PROMISE NOT TO TELL ANYONE!!
WE WON'T! GO ON, TELL US ALREADY!
OKAY, OKAY. THE GUY I HAVE A CRUSH ON IS... DIEGO!
...
...WHO?

BAH, NEVER MIND! YOU WOULDN'T KNOW HIM ANYWAY. HE'S A SENIOR.
OOKAY, THEN. LLANDRA, IT'S YOUR TURN! WHO DO YOU HAVE A CRUSH ON?
I... I'M NOT REALLY LOOKING FOR A RELATIONSHIP RIGHT NOW.
GAL!
I DIDN'T ASK IF YOU WANTED A RELATIONSHIP! I JUST WANT TO KNOW WHO YOU LIKE!
STAB
THERE... REALLY ISN'T ANYONE.
AW, COME ON! AT LEAST TELL ME WHO YOU THINK IS CUTE!
...I REALLY DON'T KNOW.
SIGH
DOUT
WELL, THIS TOPIC HAS BEEN WORTHWHILE.

YOU GUYS ARE AWARE THAT THE WINTER DANCE IS COMING UP, RIGHT?
I'LL BE HELPING TO SET IT UP.
I CAN'T WAIT! I WONDER IF I'LL GO WITH SHINJI OR HARVEY THOUGH. IT'S KIND OF TOUGH TO DECIDE...
MY SCHOOL NEVER HAS DANCES...
I THINK I JUST MAY GO WITH WHICHEVER ONE ASKS ME FIRST...
WHY ARE YOU SO WISHY-WASHY?!
WHAT?
IT'S NOT FAIR TO SHINJI OR HARVEY TO KEEP THEM GUESSING ALL THE TIME. YOU SHOULD JUST PICK ONE OR THE OTHER AND BE DONE WITH IT!
I CAN'T HELP IT IF THEY BOTH LIKE ME!
YOU'RE NOT THE CENTER OF THE UNIVERSE!
I KNEW THIS WOULD HAPPEN...

YOU GUYS! IT'S SILLY TO ARGUE ABOUT THINGS LIKE THIS!
WHAP
HEY!
GWEN! I KNOW YOU'VE NEVER BEEN TO A SLUMBER PARTY BEFORE, BUT GIRLS REALLY DON'T HAVE PILLOW-FIGHTS!
SMAK
YEAH, THAT'S THE KIND OF THING YOU ONLY SEE IN MOVIES!
AHH! STOP GANGING UP ON ME!
WHAP WHAP
WHAP
COME ON, LLANDRA! LET'S SHOW HER WHAT HAPPENS WHEN YOU START A FIGHT WITH WITCHES!
HA HA HA!
ZAP
GIGGLE
THUMP
THUMP
THUMP
AW! NO FAIR! NO MAGIC ALLOWED! AAAAH!

LATER THAT NIGHT...
I HAD A FUN NIGHT BUT WHY DID LLANDRA BLOW UP AT ME LIKE THAT? IT'S NOT FAIR FOR HER TO BE UPSET ABOUT SOMETHING I HAVE NO CONTROL OVER!
ZZZ
I CAN'T BRING MYSELF TO HURT EITHER SHINJI OR HARVEY BECAUSE I CARE ABOUT THEM BOTH...
SHE TAKES EVERYTHING SO PERSONALLY. IT HAS NOTHING TO DO WITH HER, ANYWAY!

IT JUST MAKES ME SO UPSET HOW SABRINA ACTS LIKE SHE OWNS BOTH BOYS.
THE TRUTH IS... I REALLY LIKE SHINJI. AND AS LONG AS I'M SABRINA'S BEST FRIEND, I DON'T KNOW IF I CAN TELL HER...
I WISH I COULD TELL HER...
UGHH...

I CAN'T FOCUS ON THIS TEST! WHY DO THEY ALWAYS GIVE US TESTS BEFORE IMPORTANT SOCIAL EVENTS?!
I ALREADY GOT MY DRESS... BUT I DON'T HAVE A DATE! WHY HASN'T SHINJI OR HARVEY ASKED ME YET?
Sabrina S.
Algebra
SCRIBBLE
I BET AMY SOMEHOW TRICKED HARVEY INTO AGREEING TO GO WITH HER. HE'S KIND OF GULLIBLE. AND SHINJI...HE'S A FREE SPIRIT. I BET HE'S JUST GOING TO GO SOLO.
HEH
SO IF I'M NOT ASKED BY EITHER OF THEM, IT WON'T BE BECAUSE OF ME...
...WILL IT?

HEY, 'BRINA! THE DANCE IS STILL A COUPLE OF DAYS AWAY, BUT WE'RE ALREADY GETTING THE GYM DECORATED. WANT TO HELP?
SIGN UP
FUSS FUSS
YOU SEEM UPTIGHT ABOUT SOMETHING, SABRINA.
I'M JUST STRESSING BECAUSE NEITHER SHINJI OR HARVEY HAVE ASKED ME TO THE DANCE YET. I JUST DON'T GET IT...
HAVEN'T YOU EVER THOUGHT OF ASKING EITHER OF THEM IF THEY WANT TO GO WITH YOU?
ME! NO WAY, THAT'S TOO EMBARRASSING. WHAT IF THEY TURNED ME DOWN? I'D BE MORTIFIED!
YOU COULD JUST ASK ONE OF THEM!
WHAT ABOUT MAGIC? CAN'T YOU PUT LIKE SOME KIND OF LOVE CHARM ON THEM?
IF ONLY IT WERE THAT SIMPLE. NO, LOVE CHARMS ARE STRICTLY FORBIDDEN IN MAGIC. ANY KIND OF MIND OR HEART CONTROL IS OUTLAWED.
I GUESS YOU'LL JUST HAVE TO LEARN THE HARD WAY...

THE DANCE STARTS IN 15 MINUTES. I GUESS IT'S OFFICIAL... NO ONE'S GOING TO ASK ME.
SWEETY, SHOULDN'T YOU GET GOING? YOU'RE GOING TO BE LATE FOR YOUR DANCE!
I DON'T KNOW IF I SHOULD EVEN GO...
OF COURSE YOU SHOULD GO! DON'T TELL ME YOU'RE GOING TO LET A COUPLE OF GUYS RUIN YOUR NIGHT!
BUT I DON'T HAVE A DATE! IT'S HUMILIATING.
HONEY, YOU DON'T NEED A DATE TO HAVE A GOOD TIME. BACK IN THE BAROQUE ERA, I MADE WAVES BY SHOWING UP TO THE BALL WITHOUT A MAN ON MY ARM!
THE NERVE!
GASP!
I HAD ONE OF THE BEST NIGHTS EVER. AT THE END OF THE NIGHT, HALF THE GUYS IN THE ROOM WISHED THEY WEREN'T TIED DOWN TO THEIR OWN DATES BECAUSE THEY WANTED TO DANCE WITH ME!

YEAH! I DON'T NEED A DATE! IN FACT, IF I COME ALONE THEN I CAN DANCE WITH BOTH HARVEY AND SHINJI!
I... THINK YOU MISSED MY POINT.
SMAK
WINTER DANCE TONITE
CREEAK
PEEK
THERE YOU ARE, SABRINA! I KNEW YOU'D COME!
I FEEL SO ASHAMED, GWEN. I DON'T HAVE A DATE!
NOR DO I!
I'M SORRY!
DON'T BE SORRY! I DIDN'T WANT ONE! I HAVE MORE FUN THIS WAY. COME ON, LET'S DANCE!
YIPE!

UGH, IT'S HOT IN HERE. WHERE ARE SHINJI AND HARVEY?
I DON'T BELIEVE IT!
WHO'S THAT GIRL?
I'VE NEVER SEEN HER BEFORE! COULD IT BE... HIS SECRET GIRLFRIEND?!
I NEED TO KNOW!
SABRINA! WHERE ARE YOU GOING?!
HEY, HARVEY.
HEY! THERE YOU ARE! I WAS LOOKING AROUND FOR YOU!

YOU... WERE?
YEAH, I WANTED TO INTRODUCE MY DATE TO YOU. THIS IS PENELOPE. SHE'S A FRESHMAN.
HI!!!
A FRESHMAN! WHY WOULD HARVEY DO THIS?! I THOUGHT... I THOUGHT HE LIKED ME...
SHE'S THE YOUNGER SISTER OF OUR TEAM CAPTAIN. HE ASKED ME TO TAKE HER AS A FAVOR SINCE FRESHMEN CAN'T GET INTO THE DANCE OTHERWISE.
OH... I SEE.
I GUESS I'M RELIEVED THAT IT DOESN'T MEAN ANYTHING. BUT STILL... WHY DIDN'T HE WANT TO TAKE ME AS A REAL DATE?
SIGH
WELL, WHATEVER! IT DOESN'T MATTER NOW. WHERE'S SHINJI AT?

THERE HE IS! I KNEW IT! I KNEW HE WAS COMING ALONE. HE'S SUCH A PLAYER, IT'S NO SURPRISE!
HE LOOKS BORED. I'LL GO AND KEEP HIM COMPANY. MAYBE HE'LL EVEN DANCE WITH ME!
HUH?
GIGGLE

I... DON'T BELIEVE THIS!
MY OWN BEST FRIEND! SHE... SHE BETRAYED ME! SHE KNEW SHE WAS GOING WITH SHINJI ALL ALONG!
SABRINA...
WHY WOULD LLANDRA GO BEHIND MY BACK LIKE THAT? WHY WOULD SHINJI ASK HER TO THE DANCE INSTEAD OF ME? I THOUGHT HE LIKED ME...
SABRINA...
SKTTCH

LLANDRA! YOU BETRAYED ME! HOW COULD YOU DO THIS? HOW COULD YOU BE SO SNEAKY?!
SNEAKY?! YOU WERE BEING GREEDY! WHAT MAKES YOU THINK THAT YOU HAVE ANY CLAIM TO SHINJI? HE'S HIS OWN PERSON!
I WASN'T BEING GREEDY! I JUST DIDN'T WANT TO REJECT HARVEY OR SHINJI!
YOU STILL THINK YOU HAVE BOTH BOYS WRAPPED AROUND YOUR FINGER. WELL, YOU DON'T! IF YOU WANTED THINGS TO TURN OUT DIFFERENTLY, YOU SHOULD HAVE DONE SOMETHING ABOUT IT! I DID!
WHAT ARE YOU TALKING ABOUT?
I WAS THE ONE WHO ASKED SHINJI TO THE DANCE. AND HE SAID YES.
YOU ASKED HIM?
YOU COULD HAVE ASKED HIM TOO INSTEAD OF WAITING AROUND FOR SOMETHING TO HAPPEN. SOMETIMES, IF YOU WANT SOMETHING, YOU HAVE TO GET IT YOURSELF!
...
STILL, YOU COULD HAVE TOLD ME. I MEAN, YOU DON'T EVEN GO TO THIS HIGH SCHOOL!
I KNOW... I WAS JUST AFRAID OF HOW YOU'D REACT. I GUESS I WANTED TO TEACH YOU A LESSON.

I ACTUALLY BELIEVED THAT SHINJI AND HARVEY WERE BOTH STRESSING OVER WHO WOULD BE ABLE TO TAKE ME TO THE DANCE FIRST. I GUESS...
I GUESS I'M MORE CONCEITED THAN I THOUGHT. IT HURTS BUT LLANDRA IS RIGHT. I SHOULD HAVE ASKED ONE OF THEM WEEKS AGO... I'M SO STUPID.
I SEE A COUPLE OF WALLFLOWERS HERE! COME ON, THE DANCE IS INSIDE!
COME ON, SABRINA. YOU CAN HANG OUT WITH US!
I DON'T KNOW... I'M NOT FEELING REALLY GOOD.
YOU'RE NOT ALLOWED TO SAY THAT UNTIL YOU'VE BEEN INSIDE BREATHING THE HOT, SWEATY AIR FOR AT LEAST 30 MINUTES! COME ON!
THERE YOU ARE! HOW DARE YOU RUN OFF ON ME LIKE THAT?
ARE THEY ALL PITYING ME RIGHT NOW? I DON'T WANT TO BE PITIED...

COME ON, LADIES! LET'S DANCE ALREADY!
YOU'RE SUCH A PLAYER, SHINJI!
SHINJI'S CONFIDENCE MAKES UP FOR HIS LACK OF SKILL.
COME ON! DO THE SHINJI!
I SEE WHAT YOU MEAN...
BOOGIE WOOGIE
HA HA! I GUESS HAVING THREE GOOD FRIENDS IS BETTER THAN HAVING ONE DATE WHO CAN'T DANCE!
GO ME! GO ME! IT'S MY BIRTHDAY!
OW, SHINJI! WATCH WHERE YOU'RE STEPPING!
GIGGLE
STOMP
END!!

SaLeM in
"HOUSE CAT!"

HERE YOU ARE, SALEM! YOUR VERY OWN KITTY HIGH-RISE!
AWESOME!!

THIS SEEMS LIKE A LOT OF SPACE FOR ONE CAT! I WONDER...

DING-DONG-
I'LL GET IT! IT'S PROBABLY FOR ME!
FOR YOU?!
BEEP CHIRP

RIGHT THIS WAY, PLEASE!
OKAY, WHAT'S GOING ON?

I'VE DECIDED TO CONVERT TO CONDOS!
OOH!
CONDOS FOR SALE! ONLY 2 UNITS LEFT
WE
THE END!

Chapter 6

CABIN FEVER
story & art tania del rio
inks jim amash
colors jason jensen
letters jeff powell
asst. ed. mike pellerito
editor victor gorelick
editor-in-chief richard goldwater

ONE-THOUSAND-SIX-HUNDRED AND-EIGHTY-FOUR BOTTLES OF POP ON THE WALL, ONE-THOUSAND-SIX-HUNDRED-AND-EIGHTY-FOUR BOTTLES OF POP! TAKE ONE DOWN--
SHINJI, PLEASE!
IF YOU DON'T STOP SINGING, SHINJI, I'M GOING TO MAKE HARVEY TURN THIS CAR AROUND!
I STILL DON'T SEE WHY YOU GUYS COULDN'T LET ME DRIVE US IN MY CAR! IT'S MUCH BIGGER AND FASTER, TOO!
BECAUSE THIS IS OUR TRIP TO THE CABIN, ZELDA. YOU'RE JUST HERE TO CHAPERONE!
GEE, NICE TO KNOW I'M NEEDED!
OF COURSE WE'RE HAPPY TO HAVE YOU ALONG, ZELDA! SABRINA'S JUST BEING SELFISH AS ALWAYS!

WHOSE CABIN IS THIS, ANYWAY?
I'M NOT SURE. I FOUND OUT ABOUT IT ONLINE--IT SAID THAT IT'S SPACIOUS AND NEXT TO A SKI RESORT! AND IT'S CHEAP TOO!
THAT'S WHAT I'M WORRIED ABOUT.
I'M MORE WORRIED ABOUT THE WAY THE SKY IS STARTING TO LOOK...
ONE HOUR LATER...
YEAH! WE MADE IT!
LET'S GO CHECK IT OUT, LLANDRA! LET THE BOYS HANDLE OUR THINGS!
GIGGLE!
THANKS, GIRLS.
OOF

GASP!
OH, MY.
WHAT A DUMP!
IT'S NOTHING A LITTLE MAGIC CAN'T FIX... BUT WE HAVE TO FIND A WAY TO DIVERT HARVEY'S ATTENTION. IF HE SEES IT LIKE THIS, HE'LL NEVER UNDERSTAND HOW WE MANAGED TO FIX IT UP!
SHH! THEY'RE COMING!
SLAM
UH, GIRLS. WOULD YOU MIND OPENING THE DOOR SO I CAN GET *YOUR* STUFF INSIDE?
SHINJI, THE CABIN IS A *DISASTER!* WE NEED YOU TO *DISTRACT* HARVEY SO WE CAN FIX IT UP!
WHAT?! WHY DON'T *YOU* DISTRACT HIM?

WHAT ARE YOU TALKING ABOUT? WHY AREN'T WE GOING *INSIDE?*
OH! HARVEY...
SHINJI JUST *VOLUNTEERED* TO GO TO THE GENERAL STORE WITH YOU TO PICK UP SOME *SNACKS!*
UGH
CRASH
UH, BUT... WE JUST GOT HERE! I'VE JUST BEEN DRIVING FOR *4 HOURS!*
I *KNOW,* I KNOW. BUT WE *MUST* HAVE SOME SNACKS BEFORE WE CAN SETTLE IN!
GO ON, IT WON'T TAKE LONG!
SHOVE
GLARE
GOOD, THEY'RE GONE. NOW LET'S GET TO WORK--WE *DON'T* HAVE A LOT OF TIME!

ALRIGHT, I'LL GET THE FLOORS. SABRINA GETS THE WINDOWS AND LLANDRA CAN TAKE CARE OF THE WALLS.
WHY FIX IT? AREN'T YOU SUPPOSED TO BE "ROUGHING IT"?
WE'RE JUST GOING TO MAKE THE NECESSARY REPAIRS! IT'S NOT LIKE WE'RE ADDING A HOT TUB OR ANYTHING.
ZAP
NOW TO WAIT FOR THE BOYS TO RETURN. THEN WE CAN HIT THE SLOPES!
EXCELLENT WORK, GIRLS! YOU'LL TURN INTO FINE WITCHES ONE DAY!
SPARKLE
GLEAM
MEANWHILE...
MOUNTAIN GENERAL STORE
Krisp
Chips
Poppy Corn
WACK POP
BLAST

A STRANGE TIME TO BE OUT BUYING JUNK FOOD.
WHY'S THAT?
HAVEN'T YOU HEARD? A BIG STORM'S A'BREWIN'. WISER FOLK ARE STAYING INDOORS RIGHT NOW. YOU'D BEST BE ON YOUR WAY IF YOU DON T WANT TO GET CAUGHT IN MOTHER NATURE'S FURY.
DON'T WORRY, WE'RE JUST ON OUR WAY OUT NOW.
RETURN POLICY
HOPEFULLY THE GIRLS HAVE MANAGED TO FIX UP THE PLACE BY NOW...
CRUNCH
CRUNCH

CAN'T YOU DRIVE THIS TIN CAN ANY FASTER? THE SNOW'S REALLY STARTING TO COME DOWN.
I'M DOING THE BEST I CAN, OKAY! MY CAR ISN'T USED TO THESE CONDITIONS!
UGH, IT'S GETTING HARD TO SEE.
WRRRRRRRRRRRR
WHY'D YOU STOP?!
IF YOU HAVEN'T NOTICED, I'M STILL PRESSING ON THE GAS! THE CAR'S STUCK!
WELL DON'T JUST SIT THERE! KEEP TRYING! IF WE GET STUCK NOW, WHO KNOWS WHEN WE'LL BE ABLE TO GET OUT AGAIN!
I DON'T WANT TO PUSH MY CAR TOO HARD! OTHERWISE SHE MIGHT...
KA-KA-KLUNK
...DIE.
HSSSSSS
OH, WONDERFUL!

I KNEW THIS WOULD HAPPEN! I TOLD YOU TO DRIVE FASTER!
YOU'RE BLAMING ME?!
YEAH! I'M BLAMING YOU AND YOUR RUSTED PIECE OF JUNK TOO!
HA! I'D LIKE TO SEE YOU TRY AND DRIVE THROUGH THIS WEATHER! YOU DON'T EVEN HAVE A DRIVER'S LICENSE, LET ALONE A CAR!
THAT-- THAT'S BECAUSE WHERE I COME FROM I DON'T NEED A CAR!
WHAT IS THAT SUPPOSED TO MEAN?
IT--IT'S NONE OF YOUR BUSINESS!
WELL, FINE! IF YOU DON'T NEED A CAR, THEN YOU CAN JUST WALK BACK TO THE CABIN!
MAYBE I WILL!
MAN, I COULD GET US OUT OF THIS SO EASILY WITH MAGIC. BUT I CAN'T RISK DOING ANYTHING IN FRONT OF MR. MORTAL HERE. NOT TO MENTION THAT SABRINA WOULD PUMMEL ME!

BACK AT THE CABIN...
WHAT IS TAKING THOSE BOYS SO LONG?!
THE SNOW'S REALLY PICKED UP A BIT... I HOPE THEY'RE OKAY.
WELL AT LEAST SHINJI CAN USE MAGIC IF THINGS GET BAD. I'M SURE HE'D BE ABLE TO FIND A WAY TO SNEAK A SPELL PAST HARVEY.
MAN, I'M BOOOOORED!! MAYBE WE CAN, YOU KNOW... ADD A LITTLE ENTERTAINMENT!
I WAS JUST WAITING FOR YOU TO SAY SOMETHING!
DID I EVER TELL YOU THAT I WAS ONCE A "TABLE TENNIS" MASTER BACK IN THE 1920s? WHO DARES TO CHALLENGE ME?
ZAP
I WILL! BUT NO CHEATING WITH MAGIC!
ZAP
FINE, ME AND SALEM WILL KEEP BUSY WITH THIS!
SPEAK FOR YOURSELF! I'M TOO CHILLY TO MOVE!
WHY DIDN'T YOU SAY SO? WE'LL JUST GET THE PLACE NICE AND TOASTY FOR WHEN THE BOYS ARRIVE!
ZAP

ARGH! YOU ARE SO ANNOYING!
I'M ANNOYING?! YOU'RE THE MOST OBNOXIOUS PERSON I'VE EVER MET! I DON'T KNOW WHAT SABRINA SEES IN YOU!
LIKEWISE! YOU'RE JUST A BLAND JOCK. AND YOU'RE A CHICKEN!
A CHICKEN!
FIRST OF ALL, YOU'RE TOO SCARED TO DRIVE THIS CAR LIKE A REAL MAN. SECONDLY, YOU'RE TOO CHICKEN TO TELL SABRINA HOW YOU FEEL. YOU'VE KNOWN HER FOR HOW MANY YEARS?!
AND WHAT ABOUT YOU? YOU DON'T EVEN KNOW HER! YOU JUST POP IN OUT OF NOWHERE AND THINK YOU HAVE ANY IDEA ABOUT HOW SABRINA FEELS?! GET OVER YOURSELF!
THAT'S IT! I'M DIGGING THIS CAR OUT OF HERE. I CAN'T STAND BEING STUCK IN HERE WITH YOU ANY LONGER!
WAIT! WE AGREED TO WAIT UNTIL THE STORM PASSED AND THEN DIG OUT THE CAR TOGETHER! IT'S TOO DANGEROUS OTHERWISE!
SEE? YOU'RE CHICKEN!
SLAM
ERRRGH!

IF I WORK BACK HERE MAYBE I CAN SNEAK IN A MELTING SPELL.
WOAH!
SLIP
TWACK
SHINJI!

OH, NO! THAT'S A FROZEN LAKE! THAT ICE WON'T HOLD FOR LONG!
SLIDE
GOOD SCORE!
YOU MAY BE THE PING PONG MASTER, ZELDA, BUT I'M THE VIDEOGAME MASTER!
OHHH, IF ONLY I HAD THUMBS! I'D TRIPLE YOUR SCORE, 'BRINA! I PRACTICALLY INVENTED VIDEOGAMES!
bip bip
OH, CLARICE!
THOSE BOYS REALLY ARE TAKING THEIR TIME... ARE YOU SURE WE SHOULDN'T GO LOOKING FOR THEM?
LET'S WAIT A WHILE LONGER...
I THINK IT'S TIME THOSE BOYS LEARNED TO WORK TOGETHER. THEY MIGHT ACTUALLY LEARN SOMETHING ABOUT EACH OTHER.

SHINJI! CAN YOU HEAR ME?!
UGGGH...
WOBBLE
CRACKLE
SHINJI! GET BACK DOWN! LAY ON YOUR BELLY SO YOUR WEIGHT IS DISTRIBUTED OVER THE ICE! I'M GONNA HELP PULL YOU OFF OF THERE!
THUD
GROAN...
THANK GOODNESS I HAVE THE ROPE WE USED TO TIE OUR BAGS TO THE ROOF RACK.
SWOOSH

THUD
SHINJI! CAN YOU SLIDE FORWARD AND GRAB THE ROPE?
CRACKLE
NO, SHINJI! LAY DOWN! I'M COMING TO HELP!
GOT... TO... USE MAGIC! BUT... HEAD HURTS. I'M TOO... COLD.

WHAT... IS HE... DOING? HE... HE COULD FALL THROUGH...
GRAB MY HAND! I'M ON MORE SOLID ICE, SO COME DIRECTLY TOWARDS ME!
CRAAAACK
CRRRRACK
AHHH!
DON'T PANIC! JUST MOVE TOWARDS ME! I GOT YOU!
CRASH

SIGH...
...THANKS.
DON'T MENTION IT. YOU WOULD HAVE DONE THE SAME FOR ME.
WOULD I HAVE? WOULD I RISK MY LIFE FOR HIM? *FOR ANYONE?*

NOW I KNOW WHAT SABRINA SEES IN HIM...
I'M... SORRY I CALLED YOU A CHICKEN.
HEH, IT'S OKAY. I DON'T LET STUFF LIKE THAT BOTHER ME.
HE'S A GOOD GUY. I CAN'T BELIEVE HE CAME OUT ONTO THAT THIN ICE TO HELP ME. I NEVER REALIZED HARVEY HAD IT IN HIM...
SO... NOW THAT I SEE YOU'RE BRAVER THAN I THOUGHT, HOW COME YOU HAVEN'T TOLD SABRINA HOW YOU FEEL ABOUT HER? YOU DO LIKE HER, RIGHT?
I...I, WELL, YEAH. I GUESS. YEAH.
SO WHY HAVEN'T YOU MADE A MOVE YET?
I--I GUESS I'M JUST... WAITING FOR THE RIGHT MOMENT. DON'T WANT TO MESS THINGS UP.

MESS WHAT UP? YOU'VE BEEN FRIENDS SINCE KINDERGARTEN, RIGHT? YOU CAN'T WRECK SOMETHING LIKE THAT. YOU KNOW SHE... REALLY LIKES YOU.
...YEAH?
YEAH.
MUNCH
CRUNCH
AND EVEN IF... YOU KNOW, IT DIDN'T WORK OUT, YOU'D STILL BE FRIENDS. I'M STILL FRIENDS WITH SOME OF MY EX-GIRLFRIENDS. AREN T YOU?
...I ...DUNNO.
HE'S NEVER HAD A GIRLFRIEND! NO WONDER HE'S SO FREAKED OUT ABOUT DATING SABRINA.
HE'S BEEN WAITING FOR HER HIS WHOLE LIFE.

HE HELPED ME OUT. I'M GONNA RETURN THE FAVOR. I'LL HELP HIM OUT WITH SABRINA. HE'S A GOOD GUY... HE WON'T HURT HER. I COULDN'T SAY THE SAME ABOUT ME...
I DON'T DESERVE SOMEONE LIKE SABRINA. AND SHE DESERVES SOMEONE BETTER THAN ME...
TRYING HARD TO ACT HAPPY
YOU KNOW WHAT, HARVEY, I'M GONNA HELP YOU OUT! IT'S TIME TO ACT!
WAH!
YOU LIKE HER TOO. WHY ARE YOU SO EAGER TO HELP ME ALL OF A SUDDEN?
I JUST WANT WHAT'S BEST FOR HER.
BECAUSE, I'VE BEEN HAVING A LOT OF FUN WITH LLANDRA LATELY. SHE'S A PRETTY COOL CHICK!
YOU... LIKE LLANDRA?

YEP! THAT MEANS SABRINA'S ALL YOURS, MAN. I'LL HELP YOU OUT--JUST FOLLOW MY LEAD.
GRIN
YOU'RE SCARING ME!
HMM...
YEAH... I GUESS I WILL! THANKS, SHINJI!
NO PROBLEM, 'BRO.
OKAY. YOU SAID NO HOT TUBS! NOW THIS HAS GONE TOO FAR!
STOP BEING A SOUR-PUSS! COME ON IN--THE WATER'S FINE!
UH OH. I THINK I HEAR THEM COMING!
MAGICAL ZAP-A-BUTLER©

SPLASH
QUICK! WE GOTTA ZAP ALL THIS STUFF AWAY!
SCRAMBLE
SPLASH
ZAP
ZAP
ZAP
ZAP
ZAP
creeeeak
GASP! WE... WE'RE... BACK!
WHO... WHO'S THAT DUDE?
JUST ACT NATURAL...
OH, IT'S JUST JEEVES! HE'S... UH, A BEAR-INSPECTOR! THANKS, JEEVES! THINGS LOOK GOOD HERE!
STAGGER
SHOVE

NEVER MIND THAT, WHAT TOOK YOU SO LONG?!
UH...
WELL, SABRINA, YOU WON'T BELIEVE WHAT HAPPENED! CLUMSY OLD ME STUMBLED ONTO A FROZEN LAKE. AND HARVEY ROPED ME IN INTO SAFETY LIKE A... LIKE A COWBOY!
WHY DON'T YOU TELL SABRINA ALL ABOUT IT, HARVEY?
BY THE WAY, WHERE ARE ALL THE SNACKS WE ASKED YOU TO GET?
OH! UH...WE LEFT THEM IN THE CAR.
RARRRR
MUNCH CRUNCH

SaLeM
in
"HERE'S LOOKING AT YOU!"

STARE...

IT LOOKS LIKE SALEM IS KEEPING HIS EYE ON US TONIGHT!
SO IT DOES!

SOMETIMES IT SEEMS AS IF HE REALLY KNOWS WHAT'S GOING ON!
W-WHAT DO YOU MEAN?

THE WAY HE STARES AT US, I FEEL LIKE HE'S GOT PERSONALITY, REASONING AND AN AMAZING SENSE OF INTELLIGENCE!

SNICKER SNICKER
FUNNY! I'VE NEVER FELT THAT WAY ABOUT HIM!
SIGH...
THE END

Chapter 7

Love Connections
SUN
MON
TUES
WED
THUR
FRI
SAT
29 Story & Art Tania Del Rio
30 Inks Jim Amash
31
1 Colors Jason Jensen
2
3 Letters Jeff Powell
4
5 Asst. Editor Mike Pellerito
6
7 Editor Victor Gorelick
8 REPORT DUE
9
10
11 Editor In-Chief Richard Goldwater
12 PRACTICE 3 PM
13
14 Valentine's Day
16
17
18
19
20
21
22
26
UGH...
WHY DOES VALENTINE'S DAY HAVE TO BE TOMORROW?
I'M NOT READY YET!

TOMORROW WOULD BE THE PERFECT DAY TO ASK HER OUT... BUT I WANT IT TO BE JUST RIGHT! UGH...
I COULD ASK FOR SHINJI'S HELP... HE DID SAY HE'D COACH ME THROUGH THIS.*
BUT I WANT THIS TO BE MY OWN THING!
MAN, WHAT'S THE DEAL WITH HARVEY? HE SAID HE WAS GOING TO ASK SABRINA OUT BUT IT'S BEEN OVER A MONTH AND HE STILL HASN'T DONE ANYTHING!
AW, LOOK AT HER! DOES HARVEY THINK I'M JUST GOING TO WAIT FOREVER FOR HIM TO MAKE THE FIRST MOVE?
DROOL
MAN, IT WOULD MAKE LIFE SO MUCH EASIER IF SABRINA WOULD JUST DECIDE BETWEEN US.
BUT MAYBE I'M JUST AS INDECISIVE AS SHE IS. MAYBE... MAYBE THE REASON I HAVEN'T MADE A MOVE ON SABRINA IS BECAUSE OF HOW I'M STARTING TO FEEL ABOUT LLANDRA...

MUMBLE
SNORT
MMMBRE... ANNMBR... AI... AI... NO... RENKETSU... RRRMM...
CHIRP CHIRP
YAWN

YOU'RE UP EARLY! HILDA HASN'T EVEN HAD TO USE THE FOG HORN YET!
I KNOW. I FEEL REALLY REFRESHED! BESIDES, YOU KNOW WHAT TODAY IS!
AH!
THERE'S OUR NEIGHBOR GERTA. IT LOOKS LIKE SHE'S "CASUALLY" WAITING FOR THE MAILMAN AS USUAL!
HA HA, THERE HE COMES! I WONDER IF HE HAS A VALENTINE FOR HER!-
WHAT THE--
WHAT IS IT?
CHATTER CHATTER
DON'T YOU SEE THAT? THAT "ELECTRICKY" STUFF?
WHAT? WHAT ARE YOU TALKING ABOUT?

LOOK! THOSE TWO HAVE IT TOO! IT'S LIKE SOME KIND OF CONNECTION BETWEEN THEM!
IT'S LIKE... EVERYONE IS CONNECTED TO SOMEONE... SOMEWHERE! IT'S SORT OF... ROMANTIC-LIKE!
LIKE... LIKE A LOVE CONNECTION? OOH, OOH, DO I HAVE ONE?
YEAH! BUT I'M NOT SURE WHERE IT LEADS!
WELL, WHAT ARE WE WAITING FOR? THE LOVE OF MY LIFE IS PROBABLY OUT THERE SOMEWHERE WONDERING WHY HER LIFE ISN'T COMPLETE! I'M COMING, SWEETUMS!
SORRY, SALEM. I'LL HELP YOU LOOK LATER! I'VE GOTTA GET TO SCHOOL AND SEE WHAT MY NEW POWERS CAN DO!
WELL, I MAY AS WELL USE THIS TIME TO GET READY.

OH MY GOSH! ALL THESE *CONNECTIONS!* ALL THESE LONESOME SOULS PASSING BY THEIR SOUL MATES DAY AFTER DAY WITHOUT REALIZING IT!
WELL, I'M NOT GOING TO LET THESE POWERS GO TO WASTE! TODAY I'M THE SCHOOL *CUPID!*
HMM, *UNLIKELY* COUPLE... BUT, LET'S SEE WHAT HAPPENS.

UH, DO YOU THINK YOU COULD HELP HER OUT? I WOULD, BUT I'M TOO SHORT.
UH... YEAH.
OH, THANKS!
ICE SKATE
OH, THIS IS THE FLYER FOR THE ICE-SKATING THING NEXT WEEK! I'M GOING TOO!
OH! REALLY?
H-HEY... MAYBE WE CAN GO, LIKE, TOGETHER.
YOU WANT TO GO WITH ME?! I MEAN, YEAH! SURE!
ICE SKATE
WOW...
AH!
OOF! WATCH IT!
TRIP
HERE, LET ME HELP YOU! SOME PEOPLE ARE SO RUDE!
GIGGLE

NOW WHO ELSE CAN I HELP? IT'S *VALENTINE'S DAY* AND I'M FEELING *GENEROUS!*
HMM, SHOULD I?
NAH!

SHINJI!
HI!! SHINJI!
SHINJI!
OOH!
HMPH! WHY AM I *NOT* SURPRISED?
MAN, THIS MATCHMAKING BUSINESS IS *HUNGRY* WORK!
I WONDER WHY *I* DON'T HAVE ANY CONNECTIONS...

HEY, HARVEY. YOU LOOK TERRIBLE.
THANKS. I HAVEN'T SLEPT IN DAYS.
YOU KNOW WHAT TODAY IS...
HENCE THE INSOMNIA.
ALRIGHT, COME WITH ME. WE NEED TO TALK.
I'VE BEEN UP ALL NIGHT PLANNING THE PERFECT WAY TO ASK SABRINA OUT. BUT...
BUT?
NOTHING'S... YOU KNOW, GOOD ENOUGH. I... GIVE UP.
YOU GIVE UP ?!
I'M NOT EVEN TOTALLY SURE SHE'D SAY YES. SHE STILL LIKES YOU, I KNOW SHE DOES.
LISTEN, MAN. YOU CAN'T BE ALL WISHY-WASHY. IF YOU'RE GONNA DO IT, YOU JUST GOTTA TAKE THE PLUNGE AND GO FOR IT!

I'M JUST NOT GOOD UNDER THIS KIND OF PRESSURE!
ALRIGHT. THEN LET'S PUT THE PRESSURE ON HER!
WHAT DO YOU MEAN?
TODAY'S VALENTINE'S DAY. IT'S PROBABLY THE ONLY DAY WE CAN ACTUALLY CONFRONT HER AND GET HER TO DECIDE BETWEEN US WITHOUT IT SEEMING ALL WEIRD!
HMM... YOU'RE RIGHT!
THEN LET'S ALL MEET IN HOMEROOM AFTER SCHOOL. WE'LL BOTH ASK HER TO PICK ONCE AND FOR ALL WHO SHE WANTS TO BE WITH!
ALRIGHT! THAT TAKES THE WEIGHT OFF MY SHOULDERS!
PHEW! I'M RELIEVED!
phew
I MAY STILL HAVE A CHANCE!
phew

BRRRRRRIIIING
I DID A GREAT JOB SETTING PEOPLE UP TODAY! I NEVER KNEW HOW GOOD IT FEELS TO HELP OTHERS OUT!
AW, WHAT THE HECK.
HEY. AMY WANTS TO TALK TO YOU.
HUH? WHO'S AMY?
RIGHT THERE!
SABRINA! WHAT ARE YOU DOING?
SHOVE
THIS GUY WANTED TO TALK TO YOU. BYE!
WHAT A WEIRDO!
HA HA! SOPHOMORES! WHO GETS 'EM? HEY, YOUR NAME'S AMY, RIGHT? I'M LUKE.
HII...
ZOOM

I WAS SO BUSY HELPING OTHERS... I DIDN'T REALIZE I DIDN'T GET A SINGLE VALENTINE.
I GUESS IT'S BECAUSE I DON'T HAVE A LOVE CONNECTION LIKE EVERYONE ELSE...
HEY, 'BRINA! YOU'RE LOOKING BLUE!
I DIDN'T GET ANY VALENTINES! DID YOU?
WELL, ER... A COUPLE. BUT I DON'T TAKE THEM SERIOUSLY.
I THOUGHT I'D AT LEAST GET ONE FROM HARVEY OR SHINJI...
CHEER UP. THEY WERE PROBABLY TOO SHY! GUYS AREN'T GOOD AT THAT KIND OF THING.
HERE YOU GO. YOU'VE GOT A VALENTINE NOW!
OOH! THANKS!
HAPPY VALENTINE
TA DA

SABRINA! WAIT A MINUTE!
LOOK WHO IT IS!
UHM, CAN YOU, LIKE, COME BACK TO HOMEROOM FOR A SEC?
UHHH... SURE!
WINK
MY HEART IS RACING! IS HE... IS HE GOING TO ASK ME OUT?!
UH... JUST WAIT HERE.
OHMIGOSH. WHAT'S GOING ON?!

WHAT'S TAKING SHINJI SO LONG? I CAN'T CONFRONT SABRINA WITHOUT HIS HELP!
WHAT ARE WE WAITING FOR? IS HE GOING TO MAKE A MOVE OR NOT?
WAIT A MINUTE...
MAYBE SHINJI ISN'T GOING TO SHOW UP AFTER ALL! I BET HE SET THIS UP SO ME AND SABRINA COULD BE ALONE TOGETHER! NOW, THE REST IS UP TO ME!
I'M GOING TO GO FOR IT. IT'S NOW OR NEVER. I'M GONNA TAKE THE PLUNGE!
SABRINA...

I BETTER GET TO HOMEROOM, PRONTO.
I COULD JUST "ZAP" A BOUQUET, BUT I THINK SABRINA WILL APPRECIATE THIS MORTAL EFFORT!
ANYWAY, IF SABRINA'S GOING TO DECIDE BETWEEN ME AND HARVEY, I'M GOING TO PUT SOME EXTRA EFFORT INTO SEEING THAT SHE PICKS ME!
HARVEY HAD HIS CHANCE. BESIDES, ALL'S FAIR IN LOVE AND WAR!
AT THAT MOMENT...
I-- I'VE LIKED YOU EVER SINCE I WAS LITTLE... I JUST NEVER HAD THE COURAGE TO TELL YOU.
OH, HARVEY!
FINALLY! I KNOW HOW HE FEELS ABOUT ME! I KNEW IT ALL ALONG! OH, SWEET, SHY HARVEY!

OH MY GOSH!
HEH

IT'S COOL. IT'S COOL. THEY'RE MEANT TO BE. IT'S BETTER THIS WAY. I'M HAPPY FOR THEM.
WOBBLE
I JUST DIDN'T REALIZE HOW MUCH IT'D HURT.
I CAN'T BELIEVE IT!
WE HAVE A LOVE CONNECTION! I JUST HAD TO MAKE IT HAPPEN!

ANOTHER VALENTINE'S DAY COME AND GONE...
AND ONCE AGAIN, NO VALENTINES.
IF ONLY I WENT TO SABRINA AND SHINJI'S SCHOOL. THINGS MIGHT BE *DIFFERENT*, THEN.
DING DONG
WHO'S *THAT?*
SHINJI! HI! WHAT ARE YOU DOING H--

MEANWHILE...
I'M ONE HANDSOME KITTY! MY MYSTERY GIRL WILL GO HEAD OVER HEELS FOR ME!
I'M BACK! AND YOU WON'T BELIEVE IT! HARVEY-- HE'S NOW MY... BOYFRIEND! WEEEEE!
GEL
GAL
GEE. I'M SOOOO HAPPY FOR YOU. MEANWHILE, LITTLE OLD ME HAS BEEN WAITING PATIENTLY ALL DAY TO MEET MY LOVE CONNECTION. OR DID YOU FORGET?
GIGGLE GIGGLE
WHAT? WHAT'S SO FUNNY?
YOU'VE ALREADY MET!
WHAT?!
YOUR TRUE LOVE IS YOURSELF, SALEM!
WELL, AT LEAST I'M CUTE...
GEL
END!

Chapter 8

CAUGHT ON TAPE
STORY & ART: TANIA DEL RIO | INKS: JIM AMASH | COLORS: JASON JENSEN | LETTERS: JEFF POWELL
ASSISTANT EDITOR: MIKE PELLERITO | EDITOR: VICTOR GORELICK | EDITOR-IN-CHIEF: RICHARD GOLDWATER
"The mana tree
the source of all magic
the keeper of balance
its life is our life."
-archmage Ira Hal

Treeteechi
DO YOU THINK THEY REALLY EXIST? THEY'RE LIKE A *MYTH*, RIGHT?
SHH! THE PROFESSOR IS STILL *TALKING!*
IN THE MAGIC REALM THERE ARE A NUMBER OF RARE AND MAGNIFICENT CREATURES THAT ARE *CRUCIAL* TO OUR *MAGI-STRUCTURE*. THIS IS PRECISELY WHY *MORTAL* SPORTS SUCH AS HUNTING AND TRAPPING OUR MAGICAL ANIMALS ARE *OUTLAWED*. NOW, THIS CAN HAVE ITS OWN PROBLEMS, OF COURSE--
WHISPER
GIGGLE
WHAT, SO LLANDRA CAN TALK TO *HIM* DURING CLASS AND NOT ME?!
I CAN'T EVEN *BELIEVE* THEY'RE TOGETHER. I MEAN, WHERE DID *THAT* COME FROM?! I'M JUST LIKE A *THIRD WHEEL* NOW.

I JUST WANT TO STAY IN THE MORTAL REALM SO I CAN BE WITH HARVEY...
MAN...
HOW WAS CHARM SCHOOL?
BAD. IF I DIDN'T HAVE MORTAL SCHOOL TO GO TO, I THINK I'D GO CRAZY.
WELL! AREN'T YOU BITTER! I THINK YOU SHOULD BE GRATEFUL FOR SUCH A WELL-ROUNDED EDUCATION! WHO KNOWS, YOU MAY EVEN WANT TO TAKE OVER THE WORLD ONE DAY!
ZAP
WHAT, AND END UP A FURBALL LIKE YOU? HARVEY DOESN'T LIKE CATS THAT MUCH, YOU KNOW!
HARVEY, HARVEY, HARVEY. IS THAT ALL YOU CAN TALK ABOUT THESE DAYS?
WELL, YOU DON'T HAVE TO LISTEN TO ME ANYMORE. I'M GONNA GO SEE HIM FOR A LITTLE WHILE BEFORE CURFEW. CIAO!
DON'T YOU WANT TO HANG OUT WITH ME ANYMORE?

THANKS FOR HANGING OUT WITH ME TONIGHT, HARVEY. I KNOW YOU'RE TIRED FROM BASKETBALL PRACTICE.
IT'S OKAY.
HE'S GONE BACK TO BEING SORT OF SHY AROUND ME AGAIN, BUT...
I DON'T EVER WANT THIS TO END!
THE NEXT DAY...
WAAAAAAY-HOOOOOO!!

YEEEAAAAAH!!! WOOO HOOO!!!
ACK! WHAT ARE YOU GUYS DOING?! IT'S SATURDAY!! SLEEPING-IN-DAY!
BOING
WE MADE IT!
ME-OWWW!
BOING
MADE WHAT? PANCAKES I HOPE!
NO, SILLY! I MADE IT ONTO THE MAGIC COUNCIL! THEY'RE GOING TO INAUGURATE ME TONIGHT! WE'RE ALL INVITED AND YOU'LL GET TO MEET THE QUEEN!
WOW, CONGRATS, HILDA! BUT... HARVEY AND I HAVE A DATE TONIGHT. BESIDES, I'VE ALREADY MET THE QUEEN ONCE!
GLARE
WHAT??

MAN...
WE EACH WELCOME YOU TO OUR CIRCLE. MAY YOU SERVE US AND THE PEOPLE OF THE MAGIC REALM WITH TRUTH, STRENGTH AND LOVE! DO YOU NOW ACCEPT THE POSITION OF CZARINA OF MEDIATION, AS SHE WHO MUST STRIVE TO KEEP THE MORTAL REALM APART FROM OUR OWN, YET WITHIN REACH, AT PEACE WITH OUR OWN, AND YET SECRET?
I DO.

ALL THIS COMMOTION IS MAKING ME DIZZY. I CAN'T WAIT TO GET BACK TO THE MORTAL REALM FOR SOME NORMAL, MAGIC-FREE PEACE AND QUIET!
YAK YAK
OH, AND MY ASSISTANT SHOULD HAVE YOUR NEW HOME READY BY THE END OF THE WEEK. THAT SHOULD GIVE YOU SOME TIME TO PACK YOUR MORTAL BELONGINGS.
I'VE COME TO WISH YOU GOODNIGHT, FOR IT IS TIME FOR ME TO REST. I LOOK FORWARD TO SEEING YOU IN OUR COUNCIL MEETINGS.
WH-WHAT?!
THANK YOU AGAIN, YOUR MAJESTY. GOODNIGHT.
OH, NO...
WAIT! WHAT DID SHE SAY?
THANK YOU AGAIN, YOUR MAJESTY.
SIGH...
WHAT DID SHE MEAN "NEW HOME"? WE'RE NOT MOVING!... ARE WE?
NO!

IT'S NOT FAIR! FIRST I BREAK MY DATE WITH HARVEY FOR HILDA AND NOW I HAVE TO MOVE, TOO!
WHY DOES IT HAVE TO BE NOW? HARVEY AND I HAVE JUST GOTTEN TOGETHER! NOW I'LL NEVER GET TO SEE HIM! I'LL HAVE TO STOP GOING TO MY MORTAL SCHOOL!
IT ISN'T FAIR!
PEEK
HEY, SABS... IT WON'T BE SO BAD. IT'LL BE A COOLER PLACE THAN THIS! I BET YOU THERE'LL BE A POOL AND AN ARCADE...
I DON'T CARE ABOUT THAT! HOW AM I GOING TO SEE HARVEY IF I'M ALWAYS GOING TO BE IN THE MAGIC REALM?
YOU CAN STILL VISIT ON THE WEEKENDS...
HOW WILL I EXPLAIN IT TO HIM? HE DOESN'T KNOW I'M A WITCH! I CAN'T TELL HIM WHERE I'M MOVING! HOW CAN I TELL HIM THAT I CAN ONLY MYSTERIOUSLY APPEAR ON WEEKENDS TO SEE HIM?
BESIDES, HE HAS BASKETBALL PRACTICE ON THE WEEKENDS!
WAAAAAH!

I GOT MY FIRST COUNCIL ASSIGNMENT TODAY. I WAS WONDERING IF YOU WANTED TO HELP ME OUT. CHECK OUT THE "SCENE OF THE CRIME"...
CREEEAK
YOU'RE JUST PITYING ME.
I AM NOT! I REALLY THINK I COULD USE YOUR HELP ON THIS ONE. IT'S MY FIRST ASSIGNMENT AND I DON'T WANT TO MESS UP! COME ON... PLEASE?
...FINE.
SOMEONE KIDNAPPED A TREETEECHI FROM AROUND HERE-- FOR WHAT WE DON'T KNOW. THE COUNCIL SUSPECTS IT WAS A MORTAL BECAUSE VERY FEW MAGICAL PEOPLE WOULD DO SOMETHING SO BLATANTLY UNLAWFUL AND CRAZY. IF IT WAS A MORTAL, THEN IT'S UNDER MY JURISDICTION AND I'VE GOT TO FIND HIM AND THE CREATURE A.S.A.P.
THAT'S FUNNY. I WAS JUST LOOKING AT A PICTURE OF A TREETEECHI THE OTHER NIGHT. I THOUGHT THEY WERE MAKE-BELIEVE.
LOTS OF PEOPLE DO. IT'S BECAUSE THEY'RE RATHER RARE. UNFORTUNATELY, THEY HAVE AN IMPORTANT ROLE IN OUR MAGI-SYSTEM, SO IT'S CRUCIAL THAT WE GET THIS ONE BACK BEFORE TOO MANY PROBLEMS ARISE. THE MAGIC REALM IS LIKE A POOL OF WATER... IF YOU UPSET ONE PART OF IT, THE RIPPLES SPREAD, AFFECTING EVERYTHING ELSE.

HERE WE ARE. THIS IS NEAR WHERE THE CREATURE WAS TAKEN. A PORTAL TO THE MORTAL REALM WAS ALSO OPENED HERE. OF COURSE, EVEN IF THE KIDNAPPER WAS A MORTAL, HE COULDN'T HAVE GOTTEN INTO THE MAGIC REALM HIMSELF. SOME MAGICAL PERSON MUST HAVE LET HIM IN. KEEP AN EYE OUT FOR ANY CLUES.
WELL, I SEE A BOOT-PRINT. DEFINITELY MORTAL.
HOW CAN YOU TELL?
BECAUSE IT HAS THE "GLOSSY" LOGO. THAT'S A REALLY POPULAR BRAND IN THE MORTAL REALM.
SEE? I KNEW IT'D BE GOOD TO BRING YOU ALONG!
THAT STILL DOESN'T TELL US MUCH, THOUGH.
OH! WHAT'S THIS?
WEIRD. IT LOOKS SORT OF LIKE THE PRINT OF A TWIGGY-BIRD. MAYBE HE KIDNAPPED OTHER ANIMALS TOO!

WELL, FROM THE BOOT WE KNOW KIDNAPPER WAS PROBABLY MORTAL. THE QUESTION IS, WHO LET HIM INTO THE MAGIC REALM? IF WE CAN FIND THAT PERSON, WE CAN GET SOME ANSWERS.
I'D GUESS A FRIEND OF HIS. ANOTHER HUNTER. MY PROFESSOR SAID THAT MAGICAL PEOPLE OFTEN GO TO THE MORTAL REALM TO HUNT SINCE THEY CAN'T DO IT IN THE MAGIC REALM. I BET YOU SOME OF THEM BECOME FRIENDS WITH THE MORTAL HUNTERS.
THAT'S RIGHT. THERE'S AN ORGANIZATION CALLED "MAGICAL HUNTERS OF THE MORTAL REALM" I'LL GET A LIST FROM THE COUNCIL RECORDS AND WE'LL TALK TO EACH MEMBER. LUCKILY THERE AREN'T MANY.
3 HOURS LATER...
KNOCK KNOCK
131
WELL, WE'VE ALREADY QUESTIONED 7 MEMBERS WITH NO LUCK. THERE ARE ONLY 4 MORE TO GO... IF NOTHING TURNS UP, I DON'T KNOW WHAT WE'LL DO.
H-HELLO?
HELLO. I'M HILDA SPELLMAN, CZARINA OF MEDIATION. MAY I COME IN?
I DON'T KNOW WHAT YOU'RE TALKING ABOUT. I'M NOT A CRIMINAL! I DON'T WANT ANY TROUBLE, OKAY?
I SEE. WELL, THANK YOU FOR YOUR TIME.

UGH, 3 MORE TO GO. I COULD BE HANGING OUT WITH HARVEY RIGHT NOW WATCHIN A VIDEO OR SOMETHING.
A VIDEOTAPE! WHY WOULD SOMEONE LIVING IN THE MAGIC REALM HAVE ONE OF THOSE LAYING AROUND?! MAGI-DISCS ARE SO MUCH BETTER!
WAIT A MINUTE! THE MARKS WE SAW AT THE SCENE.. THAT WAS THE INDENTATION OF A TRIPOD-- NOT A BIRD! ONLY MORTALS USE TRIPODS FOR MORTAL VIDEO CAMERAS-- AND MORTAL VIDEOTAPES. THIS GUY MUST HAVE A CONNECTION!
WHISPER WHISPER
MR.SNIPLEY, BEFORE WE GO, MAY I ASK WHY YOU HAVE A MORTAL VIDEOTAPE IF YOU HAVE NO VCR TO PLAY IT ON?
L-LOOK, IT ISN'T MINE OKAY? A FRIEND LEFT IT FOR ME. I WANT NOTHING TO DO WITH HIM OR HIS STUPID ACTIONS. I DON'T WANT ANY TROUBLE! I GOT A FAMILY!

ARE YOU *IMPLYING* THAT THIS TAPE HAS SOMETHING TO DO WITH THE KIDNAPPING OF THAT *TREETEECHI?*
LOOK, *PLEASE* DON'T PIN THIS ON ME. THAT CRAZY MORTAL GAVE IT TO ME AND SAID, "I'M PITCHING THIS TO THE EXECS-- WE'LL BE *RICH!*" I DON'T EVEN KNOW WHAT *"PITCHING TO EXECS"* MEANS!
DID *YOU* LET THIS MORTAL INTO THE MAGIC REALM, MR. SNIPLEY? IT *APPEARS* HE'S TRYING TO PAY YOU BACK FOR *SOMETHING.*
LOOK, LET ME GO. KEEP THE *TAPE,* I'LL EVEN TELL YOU HIS NAME. BUT *PLEASE* LET ME GO. I DIDN'T THINK HE WAS GOING TO *STEAL* FROM THE MAGIC REALM. REALLY! I *TRUSTED* HIM! NOW, I WANT *NOTHING* TO DO WITH HIM! HIS NAME IS *ATTICUS REX.* JUST LET ME BE! PLEASE.
THIS IS YOUR FIRST AND *LAST* WARNING, MR. SNIPLEY.
UGH
YEAH! IF *I'M* NOT EVEN ALLOWED TO LET MY *BOYFRIEND* INTO THE MAGIC REALM, WHY SHOULD *YOU* BE ABLE TO LET *CRIMINALS* IN?
SABRINA, *PLEASE!* LET ME HANDLE THIS.
DYAH
BACK AT THE COUNCIL HALL...

I JUST WANTED TO SHOW YOU THIS KEY PIECE OF EVIDENCE BEFORE I WENT ANY FURTHER WITH THIS. I ALSO HAVE THE NAME OF THE CRIMINAL. ATTICUS REX.
WH-WHAT IS THIS STRANGE DEVICE?
IS THERE SOMETHING INSIDE? IS IT A BOX OF SOME SORT?
THAT'S A HAIR-CURLING TOOL, I BELIEVE.
ACTUALLY... IT'S A VIDEOTAPE. I'M GOING TO HAVE TO GO TO THE MORTAL REALM TO VIEW IT ON MY VCR AT HOME. I'LL SEE IF I CAN GET MORE INFO FROM THAT.
VEE-SEE-ARR?
UH... JUST LEAVE IT TO ME!

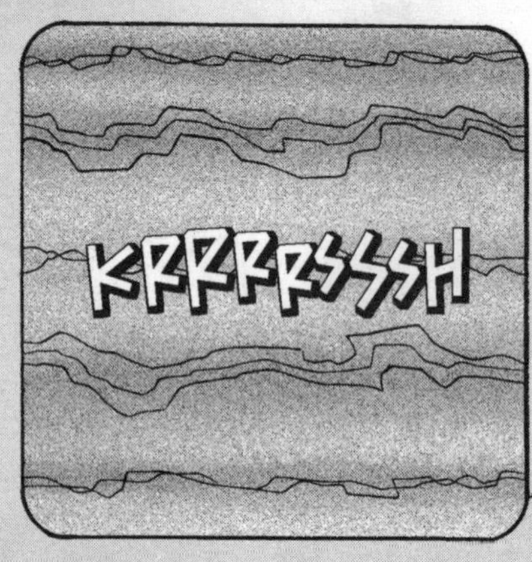
KRRRRSSSH

`ALLO! ATTICUS REX, BEAST-CATCHER HERE! I'M HERE TO PITCH ONE OF THE HOTTEST SHOWS YOU NETWORKS WILL EVER HAVE THE PLEASURE OF SEEING!
PFFFT!
SHH!

IM A HUNTER BY TRADE AND I SPECIALIZE IN CAPTURING EXCEPTIONALLY RARE AND DEADLY BEASTS SUCH AS THIS ONE...

THE GREEN-LEECHER! A FEARSOME BEAST THAT I TACKLED DEEP IN THE JUNGLES OF AN EXOTIC LAND. TAKE A LOOK!
HEY! THERE IT IS! THAT'S THE--
YES, YES. KEEP WATCHING.

REPLAY

HAH!

ARGH! GRUNT! ERK! COME HERE YOU MANGY MONSTER!
CRUNCH
SNAP

GOT 'IM!

MY SHOW WILL TAKE YOU ON A WILD ADVENTURE AS YOU FOLLOW ME, ATTICUS REX, BEAST-HUNTER, INTO PLACES NO MAN HAS WALKED BEFORE! WATCH ME CHASE DOWN AND CAPTURE ALL KINDS OF RARE AND TERRIBLE CREATURES LIKE THIS ONE!
FOR ONLY I CAN SPEAK THEIR MONSTROUS LANGUAGE. ONLY I CAN RULE THEM ALL!

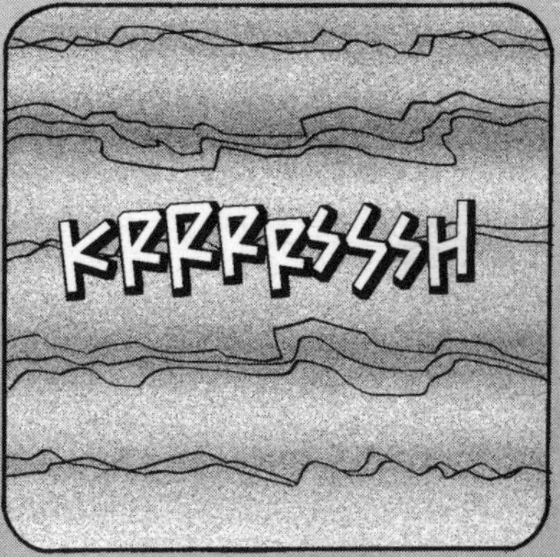
KRRRRSSSH

I CAN'T TAKE ANYMORE.
OH NO... HE'S PROBABLY ALREADY SENT THIS TAPE OUT TO A BUNCH OF NETWORKS--WHICH MEANS MORTALS HAVE PROBABLY ALREADY SEEN THE TREETEECHI! WORSE YET, THESE NETWORKS MIGHT EVEN BE INTERESTED!
THAT GIVES ME AN IDEA.

IS THIS ATTICUS REX, BEAST HUNTER?
WHO'SIS?
MY NAME IS HILDA SPELLMAN AND I'M PRESIDENT OF THE ANIMAL-TASTIC CHANNEL. I MUST SAY I'M VERY INTERESTED IN YOUR DEMO TAPE. I'M TALKING 7-DIGITS INTERESTED!
NOW WE'RE TALKIN'!! I ALWAYS KNEW I WAS BORN TO BE A STAR!
YES, IN FACT WE WANT YOU TO SIGN A CONTRACT WITH US TONIGHT-- BEFORE ANY OTHER NETWORKS CATCH ON, YOU SEE!
W-WELL SURE! 7 DIGITS, YOU SAY? I'M ALL FOR THAT!
OF COURSE, YOU MUST BRING THE CREATURE ALONG. WE HAVE TO MAKE SURE IT'S REAL BEFORE WE COMMIT TO ANYTHING.
GOTTA BRING OVER A BIT OF EXTRA PROTECTION. WHO'S TO SAY THEY'RE NOT TRYING TO SET ME UP SO THEY CAN STEAL THIS UGLY BEAST--AND MY GLORY!

I CAN'T BELIEVE I HAVE TO DO THIS. I'VE LIVED HERE ALMOST ALL MY LIFE... I MET HARVEY HERE...
STUFF
BEDROOM
MAGAZINES
STUFF
SABRINA! ARE YOU READY TO NAB THIS GUY? COME ON!
YEAH...
WOW, I DIDN'T KNOW YOU COULD CONJURE UP A PLACE LIKE THIS, HILDA. THAT TAKES A LOT OF SKILL-- ESPECIALLY IN THE MORTAL REALM!
HEE HEE! WHAT CAN I SAY?
KNOCK KNOCK
COME IN!
'LO.

SO YOU LIKED MY PITCH HUH? I DON'T BLAME YOU--I WAS BORN TO BE STAR. I HAVE CHARISMA!
YES INDEED! NOW, TELL ME WHERE YOU GOT THIS CREATURE.
WELL, THAT'S MY LITTLE SECRET. LET'S SAY I HAVE MY OWN SOURCE FOR A VARIETY OF RARE MONSTERS LIKE THIS ONE.
IT'S NOT AN ILLEGAL SOURCE, IS IT?
I WOULDN T WORRY YOURSELF WITH THAT. LEAVE THE CREATURE HANDLING TO ME--YOU WORRY ABOUT THE RATINGS!
YES, YES! THE RATINGS! NOW, MAY WE SEE THE CREATURE?
HEH
OOOOH!!!
GET A GRIP, SABRINA!

WELL THAT CINCHES IT. YOU'RE THE MAN!
ALRIGHT! IS IT TIME TO SIGN THIS MILLION-DOLLAR CONTRACT?
CLICK
WRONG!
ZAP
WAH! WHAT'S GOING ON HERE?
A MORTAL LIKE YOU SHOULD NEVER HAVE BEEN LET INTO THE MAGIC REALM. I'M GOING TO ENSURE YOU NEVER GO BACK TO STEAL ANY MORE OF OUR WONDERFUL CREATURES!
YOU TRICKED ME!
NOW, THIS CREATURE IS GOING BACK TO WHERE IT BELONGS. YOU, ON THE OTHER HAND, WILL HAVE YOUR MEMORY WIPED. YOU'LL BE ABLE TO LIVE YOUR LIFE AS THOUGH THIS NEVER HAPPENED. YOU SHOULD THANK US FOR THE CHANCE TO LIVE YOUR LIFE ANEW.
NO!
LET ME GO!
GASP!
NO! LET HER GO!

YOU LOSER! I'VE BEEN HAVING A VERY BAD WEEK! YOU'RE GOING TO REGRET MAKING IT WORSE!
SABRINA, NO!
BLAST ZAP
ARGGH! YOU WITCH!
RRRGGGGHH
WHAT THE--?
ERRRRGGGGHH
EEK
THE TREETEECHI! IT'S TRANSFORMED INTO ITS GUARDIAN FORM! BUT ONLY A FULL MOON CAN DO THAT! BUT THE MOON'S WANING RIGHT NOW!
AHHH!
WHA--?

ARRGGH! LET ME GO!
RRRGGGGHH
LET'S SEE IF YOU CAN WRANGLE SOMETHING BIGGER THAN A TEDDY BEAR. THEN WE MAY HAVE A SHOW!
SOON...
EXCELLENT WORK, HILDA. YOU DID NOT DISAPPOINT. AS FOR YOU, MR. REX, YOU WILL WAKE UP WITH NO MEMORY OF THIS UNPLEASANT EVENT.
OH, DON'T BE SO SURE. I'LL REMEMBER THIS--WITH EVERY FIBER OF MY BEING! MARK MY WORDS! YOU WITCHES TOOK AWAY MY CHANCE TO BE A STAR! YOU'LL PAY FOR THAT!
SABRINA?
WHAT?
WE DON'T HAVE TO MOVE! THE COUNCIL REALIZED I CAN DO MY JOB JUST AS WELL--IF NOT BETTER--FROM RIGHT HERE IN THE MORTAL REALM. AND IT'S ALL BECAUSE OF THAT SILLY VIDEOTAPE THEY COULDN'T COMPREHEND!

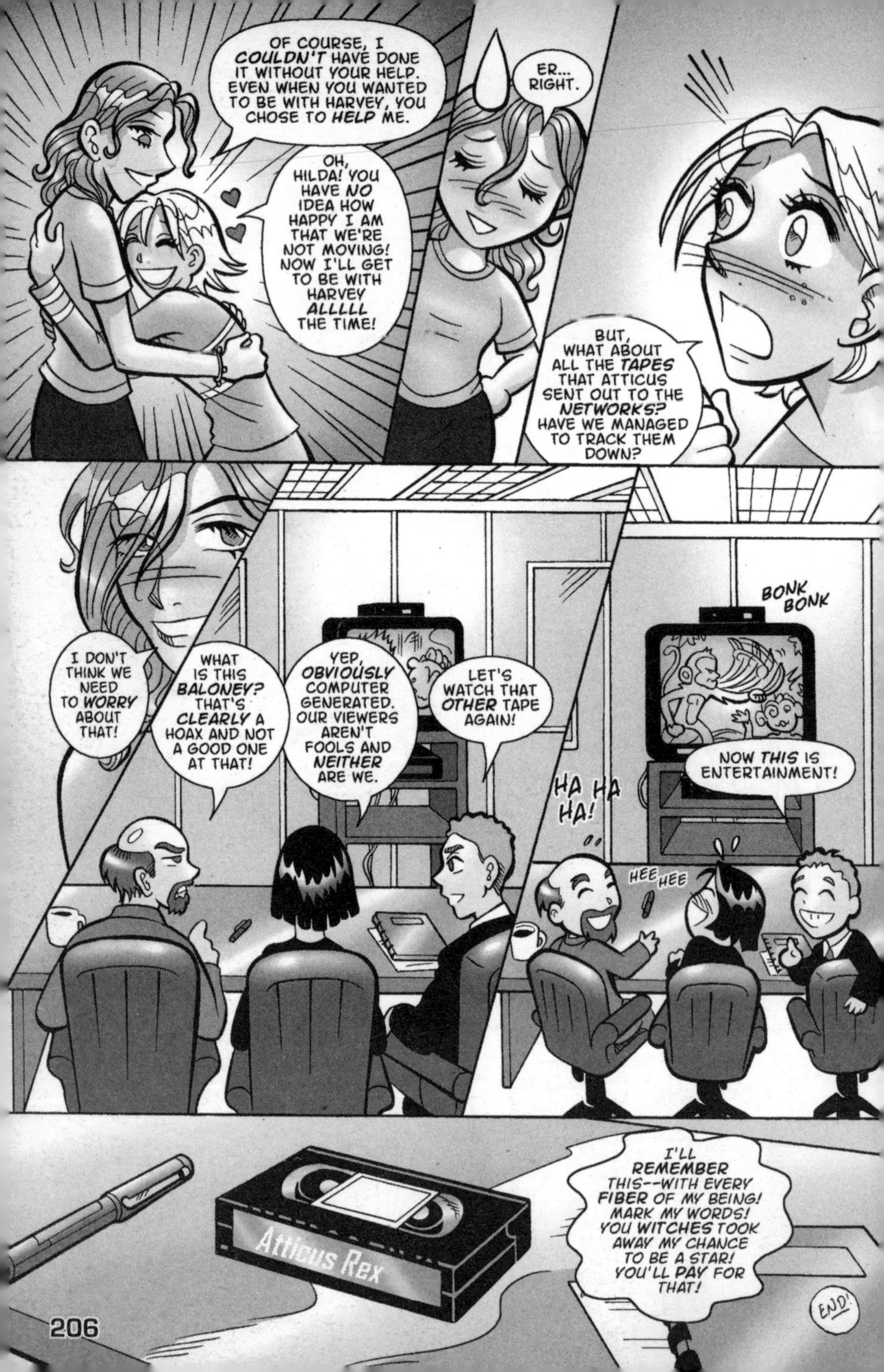
OF COURSE, I COULDN'T HAVE DONE IT WITHOUT YOUR HELP. EVEN WHEN YOU WANTED TO BE WITH HARVEY, YOU CHOSE TO HELP ME.
OH, HILDA! YOU HAVE NO IDEA HOW HAPPY I AM THAT WE'RE NOT MOVING! NOW I'LL GET TO BE WITH HARVEY ALLLLL THE TIME!
ER... RIGHT.
BUT, WHAT ABOUT ALL THE TAPES THAT ATTICUS SENT OUT TO THE NETWORKS? HAVE WE MANAGED TO TRACK THEM DOWN?
I DON'T THINK WE NEED TO WORRY ABOUT THAT!
WHAT IS THIS BALONEY? THAT'S CLEARLY A HOAX AND NOT A GOOD ONE AT THAT!
YEP, OBVIOUSLY COMPUTER GENERATED. OUR VIEWERS AREN'T FOOLS AND NEITHER ARE WE.
LET'S WATCH THAT OTHER TAPE AGAIN!
BONK BONK
HA HA HA!
HEE HEE
NOW THIS IS ENTERTAINMENT!
Atticus Rex
I'LL REMEMBER THIS--WITH EVERY FIBER OF MY BEING! MARK MY WORDS! YOU WITCHES TOOK AWAY MY CHANCE TO BE A STAR! YOU'LL PAY FOR THAT!
END!

Chapter 9

SALEM MANIA
Story & Art TANIA DEL RIO
Inks JIM AMASH
Colors JASON JENSEN
Letters JEFF POWELL
Assistant Editor MIKE PELLERITO
Editor VICTOR GORELICK
Editor-In-Chief RICHARD GOLDWATER
I COULD LOOK AT MYSELF ALL DAY!
Gloss
MAN!
WHAT'S WRONG NOW?
HE'S BUSY AGAIN. EVER SINCE WE'VE GOTTEN TOGETHER IT SEEMS LIKE HARVEY'S BEEN TRYING TO AVOID ME MORE AND MORE!
WELL, DON'T YOU HAVE SOME HOMEWORK OR SOMETHING THAT CAN KEEP YOU BUSY INSTEAD?
IT'S FRIDAY NIGHT! MAN, YOU'RE STARTING TO SOUND LIKE AUNT HILDA!
OOOH, DON'T SAY THAT! AH, WHAT HAS BECOME OF ME? I USED TO CONTROL MAGICAL ARMIES AND NOW I'M REDUCED TO BEING A TEEN COUNSELOR!
MORE LIKE A TEEN NAGGER.

HA HA. WELL, WHY DON'T YOU CALL UP LLANDRA?
OHHH, I CAN'T.
WHY NOT?
BECAUSE SHE'S GOING OUT WITH SHINJI NOW AND THEY'RE ALWAYS TOGETHER. IT'S WEIRD. BESIDES, WHEN I HANG OUT WITH THEM THEY ACT LIKE I'M INVISIBLE.
SIGH... I GIVE UP.
I'LL GET IT!
WAH
CHIRP CHIRP
SHINJI! HI! YOU HAVEN'T CALLED ME IN AGES! ...WHAT? UH... SURE. I GUESS.
WELL, HAS YOUR FRIDAY NIGHT BEEN SAVED?
HMM
SORT OF. SHINJI ASKED ME TO HELP HIM MOVE INTO AN APARTMENT IN GREENDALE! BUT I THOUGHT HE LIVED IN THE MAGIC REALM!

THANKS FOR COMING, GUYS. WE NEED ALL THE HELP WE CAN GET TO MOVE INTO THIS NEW APARTMENT *ASAP!*
WHY DID YOU DECIDE TO LEAVE THE MAGIC REALM?
WE *DIDN'T.* THIS APARTMENT IS JUST A *RUSE.* OUR UNCLE FROM JAPAN HAS DECIDED THAT HE WANTS TO COME VISIT US. HE'S JUST A *MORTAL,* SO HE DOESN'T KNOW ANYTHING ABOUT THE MAGIC REALM. OF COURSE, HE COULDN'T COME VISIT US *THERE,* SO WE HAD TO COME UP WITH SOME KIND OF PLAN QUICKLY! AND HERE WE ARE.
THIS IS KIND OF SHORT NOTICE SO WE NEED A BIT OF EXTRA MAGICAL HELP TO GET THIS APARTMENT IN ORDER. BUT WE HAVE TO BE *CAREFUL.* THE WALLS ARE THIN AND WE HAVE TO BE SUBTLE WITH OUR MAGIC. *NO* BIG ZAPS!
ZAP
ZAP
CHATTER
GIGGLE
HOW *NICE.* SHINJI ONLY CALLS ME WHEN HE *NEEDS* SOMETHING AND THEN HE SPENDS THE WHOLE TIME *IGNORING* ME AS USUAL.
WHAT *HAPPENED?* HE USED TO BE *SO* NICE TO ME... THE WAY HE ACTS AROUND LLANDRA... I WISH *HARVEY* WERE MORE LIKE HIM.
I MEAN, NO I DON'T!

WELL!
I MUST SAY, YOU ALL DID A GOOD JOB PULLING THIS PLACE TOGETHER! OF COURSE, IF I STILL HAD MY MAGIC, IT'D BE A TAD TRENDIER BUT, EH, WE CAN'T ALL HAVE A CAT'S COOL!
KONNICHI WA!*
*JAPANESE FOR "HELLO!" – ED
Y-YOJI-SAN! YOU'RE HERE!
YES, I DECIDED TO GO AHEAD AND TAKE THE EARLY FLIGHT. SURPRISE!
EEP
WHAT A REMARKABLE CAT!
HE DIDN'T HEAR ME SPEAK, DID HE?
HE'S JUST A REGULAR CAT! IT'S NOT LIKE HE CAN TALK OR ANYTHING!
WELL, OF COURSE HE CAN'T TALK! BUT HE IS THE MOST ADORABLE CAT I'VE EVER SEEN! HE'D BE DELIGHTFUL IF STUFFED!
INTERCEPTION!
PLEASE DON'T STUFF ME!

SEE, THIS IS EXACTLY WHY I CAME HERE TO AMERICA--FOR INSPIRATION! AND TO SEE MY NEPHEWS, OF COURSE!
UH, YES. UNCLE YOJI IS A TOY DESIGNER IN TOKYO.
SQUEEEEEZE
HOW SOFT! ANY CHILD WOULD LOVE TO CUDDLE HIM IN THEIR ARMS!
POKE POKE
POKE ME ONE MORE TIME...
OW!
MEOW! HOW CUTE! WHAT A LOVELY LITTLE KITTY!
YANK
UH... YEP. HE'S ONE OF A KIND!
HMMM...
WHA?
WELL, THANKS FOR STOPPING BY, SABRINA! I'M SURE UNCLE YOJI WANTS TO REST AFTER HIS LONG FLIGHT. OH, AND DON'T FORGET YOUR, UH, CAT!

THAT JERK! I COME OVER TO HELP HIM AND HE CAN'T WAIT TO GET RID OF ME!
GRRRR
ATER THAT NIGHT...
SO WHAT WAS UP WITH YOUR BOYFRIEND TREATING ME LIKE THAT?
WHAT DO YOU MEAN?
YOU KNOW EXACTLY WHAT I MEAN! HE LITERALLY SHOVED ME OUT OF THE APARTMENT!
HE... WAS JUST NERVOUS ABOUT SALEM. HE DIDN'T WANT HIS UNCLE TO CATCH ON THAT SALEM WAS MAGICAL. AND, LIKE HE SAID, HIS UNCLE NEEDED TO REST.
THEN WHY DIDN'T HE KICK YOU OUT TOO?
I GUESS HE WANTED TO FORMALLY INTRODUCE ME... AS HIS GIRLFRIEND. THEN WE ALL HAD DINNER.
WHY DO I FEEL SO... JEALOUS? I HAVE HARVEY NOW! HE'S THE ONE I LOVE!
HE NEXT DAY...

PLEASE, SALEM?
NO! I ALREADY HELPED YOU OUT IN HISTORY CLASS. I'M NOT GOING TO HELP YOU IN CALCULUS, TOO!
SHH-- SOMEONE'S COMING!
AREN'T YOU GETTING A LITTLE OLD TO BRING STUFFED TOYS TO SCHOOL?
AREN'T YOU GETTING A LITTLE OLD TO PICK ON SOPHOMORES?
SO WHERE'S HARVEY? CONSIDERING HE'S SUPPOSEDLY YOUR BOYFRIEND, I HARDLY EVER SEE YOU TWO TOGETHER.
HE IS MY BOYFRIEND.
IS THAT WHAT YOU THINK? HOW CUTE.
WHAT ARE YOU TALKING ABOUT?
OH, NOTHING. IT'S JUST WHEN I ASKED HARVEY THE OTHER DAY IF YOU TWO WERE TOGETHER HE SAID "NOT REALLY". HMM, I WONDER WHAT THAT COULD MEAN?

SIGH...
HARVEY!
HI, HARVEY!
UH... HI.
SNICKER
SNICKER
EXIT
CAN I... TALK TO YOU FOR A MINUTE?
UH OH, HARVEY! YOU'RE IN TROUBLE, NOW!
HEH
SNICKER SNICKER
I HAVE TO GET TO CLASS. WHAT IS IT?
IT'S JUST... UM...
IT'S... NOTHING. NEVER MIND.
OKAY. WELL, SEE YA. GUYS, WAIT UP!

SEVERAL WEEKS LATER...
Well, I still haven't gotten the courage to confront Harvey about what Amy said. I guess I'm afraid that if I bring it up, he'll admit that it's true. I'd rather go on believing that we're really together...
But he hasn't kissed me since Valentine's Day. He barely even holds my hand. Did I do something wrong?
EEEEE! SABRINA, LOOK AT THIS!
AAAH!
ISN'T IT CUTE?! IT'S LIKE SALEM-- ONLY HAPPIER AND CUDDLIER AND LESS CYNICAL!
I LOOOOOOVE YOU! TEE HEE!
AAAAAAAAAH! WHERE DID YOU FIND THAT ABOMINATION?!

HAVEN'T YOU HEARD? IT'S THE HOT NEW THING FROM JAPAN! IT LOOKS LIKE SALEM BUT IT'S CALLED MISTER KITTY-LITTER! THERE'S ALL KIND OF MERCHANDISE OUT!
MISTER KITTY-LITTER?!! MY IMAGE HAS BEEN TAINTED! AND MY EARS AREN'T THAT BIG-- ARE THEY? HOW IS THIS POSSIBLE?!
YOJI YAMAGI!
I CAN'T BELIEVE IT! SALEM! YOU'RE EVERYWHERE!

WOW, AMY! YOU HAVE ALL THE NEWEST MISTER KITTY LITTER ACCESSORIES! I'VE BEEN DYING TO FIND THAT BAG!
WELL, I LIKE TO KEEP UP WITH THE LATEST STYLES!
LATEST STYLES?! I'M THE ONE WHO STARTED THIS FAD! I'VE BEEN BRINGING THE ORIGINAL SA-- ER-- MISTER KITTY LITTER TO SCHOOL FOR YEARS! YOU ALL COPIED ME!
I CAN NOT BELIEVE THIS ARGUMENT IS TAKING PLACE.
HOW PATHETIC. AS IF ANYONE WOULD WANT TO COPY YOU. ALL YOU HAVE IS THE STUFFED TOY. YOU'RE NOT EVEN TRENDY ENOUGH TO HAVE ALL THE ACCESSORIES! AS USUAL, YOU'RE A LITTLE SLOW TO CATCH ON, SABRINA.
ERRRGH! WHO DOES SHE THINK SHE IS? LIKE I WANT TO BE CAUGHT DRESSED IN ANYTHING SHE WEARS, ANYWAY! SORRY, SALEM, BUT I CAN'T BRING YOU TO SCHOOL ANYMORE. YOU'RE JUST TOO POPULAR AND I DON'T WANT TO LOOK LIKE I'M JUST A COPY-CAT.
SIGH...
STORM STORM
LATER...
WOW, SALEM! LOOK, YOU'RE ON A COMMERCIAL!

THE NEW MISTER KITTY LITTER DOLL COMES WITH HIS OWN SPARKLY LITTER BOX! BUT--OOPS! HE'S STILL LEARNING! TIME TO PUT ON HIS DIAPER!
THERE, THERE, MISTER KITTY LITTER, DON'T CRY. I'M SURE YOU'LL BE LITTER-TRAINED IN NO TIME!
I LOVE YOU, MISTER KITTY LITTER!
MEOW MEOW!
TURN IT OFF! TURN IT OFF! THE HORROR!
WELL, AT LEAST YOU'RE FAMOUS!
FAMOUS?! FAMOUS?! FAMOUS FOR BEING A CHILD'S PLAYTHING--FOR BEING A FAD! I WANTED TO BE KNOWN FOR MY MAGICAL PROWESS--FOR THE WAY THE WORLD TREMBLED WHEN I TRIED TO CONQUER IT! I WANT TO BE KNOWN FOR WHO I WAS!
...NOT WHO I'VE BECOME...

JAPANESE IMPORT
MR. KITTY LITTER TAKES
AMERICA BY STORM
Kitty Kola
NEW!
MISTER KITTY LITTER
MISTER
KITTY LITTER
MOVIE
MR. KITTY LITTER NOW
CHILDREN'S MOST
RECOGNIZED CHARACTER
KITTY
MR. KITTY LITTER CRAZE IS
"LITTER-ALLY" THE HOTTEST
THING THIS YEAR
FOOD
SNACK
DRINK
KITTY LITTER
LAND

I NEVER THOUGHT I'D SAY THIS, BUT...
I'M SICK OF LOOKING AT MYSELF!
SABRINA! YOU'VE GOT TO HELP ME!
WHAT CAN I POSSIBLY DO?!
TALK TO SHINJI! ASK HIM TO TELL HIS UNCLE TO STOP WITH THE MISTER KITTY LITTER STUFF. SAY I'LL THREATEN TO SUE! ANYTHING! JUST SO IT STOPS!
I... DON'T KNOW, SALEM. THIS HAS ALL GOTTEN SO BIG I DOUBT SHINJI'S UNCLE WOULD BE WILLING TO GIVE IT UP JUST LIKE THAT.
PLEEEEEEASE?
SIMPER
OH, SALEM! DON'T LOOK AT ME LIKE THAT! OKAY, FINE! I'LL TALK TO SHINJI! BUT I DON'T THINK IT'S GOING TO MAKE A DIFFERENCE.
HEH HEH.
WORKS EVERY TIME!
MORE THAN ANYTHING, I'M JUST SCARED TO TALK TO SHINJI. HE'S BEEN SO STRANGE WITH ME LATELY...

HI, SHINJI. IT'S SABRINA. UM... I WAS WONDERING IF WE COULD MEET SOMEWHERE TO TALK.
I... DUNNO. I'M KIND OF BUSY.
UGH, HE SOUNDS LIKE *HARVEY*.
PLEASE, SHINJI? IT WON'T TAKE LONG. IT'S ABOUT *SALEM*. I'LL EVEN MEET YOU IN THE MAGIC REALM.
SIGH... FINE. I'M HANGING OUT WITH LLANDRA NOW BUT WE CAN TALK LATER TONIGHT.
LLANDRA'S *LUCKY* TO HAVE A GUY WHO *LIKES* SPENDING TIME WITH HER...
Shinji

THANKS FOR MEETING WITH ME, SHINJI. I KNOW YOU PROBABLY DIDN'T WANT TO LEAVE LLANDRA.
...
SO WHAT'S THE EMERGENCY?
N-NO EMERGENCY, REALLY. IT'S JUST...
WHY AM I SO NERVOUS?! I'VE NEVER FELT THIS NERVOUS AROUND SHINJI BEFORE! MY LIPS ARE ALL DRY... IT'S A GOOD THING I BROUGHT LIP GLOSS.
IT'S ABOUT SALEM...
STRAWBERRY LIP GLOSS. YOUR FAVORITE, HUH?
WHAT? HOW WOULD YOU KNOW?
I SAW YOU EATING SOME IN CLASS ONE NIGHT.
I--I DID NOT!
STRAWBERRY
Gloss
HA HA! I SAW YOU! I DIDN'T SAY ANYTHING AT THE TIME BUT I THOUGHT IT WAS HILARIOUS! BUT IT'S OKAY. I BET IT TASTES GOOD.
I MEAN... ER... NOT THAT I WOULD EVER TASTE YOUR STRAWBERRY LIP GLOSS. I MEAN, I WOULDN'T KNOW.
AWKWARD SILENCE

ANYWAY... ABOUT SALEM. HE WAS HOPING YOU COULD TALK YOUR UNCLE OUT OF MAKING ANY MORE MISTER KITTY LITTER STUFF. IT'S BEEN REAL TOUGH ON HIM SEEING HIS IMAGE EVERYWHERE.
I DUNNO... MY UNCLE SAYS IT'S HIS BEST HIT YET. BUT I'M SURE THE CRAZE WILL DIE DOWN ON ITS OWN.
I KNOW. IT'S SILLY TO ASK. BUT SALEM SEEMED SO UPSET THAT I FELT LIKE I NEEDED TO TRY AT LEAST. WILL YOU AT LEAST SPEAK TO YOUR UNCLE? EVEN IF HE DOESN'T AGREE?
UH, SURE. I GUESS. BUT, LIKE I SAID, I DOUBT IT WILL DO ANYTHING.
THANKS, SHINJI! THAT'S ALL I WANTED TO HEAR!
UHH...
HUG
I MEAN... SALEM WILL BE HAPPY...
ZOOM
ZOOM

NOOOOO...
LOOM
CRUNCH
NOOOO! SAVE MEEEEEE!
LOOK AT YOU! FEH. PATHETIC.
WHAT HAVE YOU BECOME? A SNIVELING LITTLE KITTY! WE SHOULD BOTH BE ASHAMED!
HUH?
Y-YOU!

WHO HAVE YOU BECOME? THE SALEM I KNOW WOULDN'T GET ALL WORKED UP OVER A LITTLE OBSTACLE. THE SALEM I KNOW WOULD TAKE LEMONS AND MAKE POISON-LEMONADE! WHAT HAPPENED TO THE SALEM WHO TOOK ADVANTAGE OF EVERY SITUATION AND DIDN'T LET ANYTHING BRING HIM DOWN?
I... I...
YOU? DON'T YOU MEAN "ME"? COME ON, DON'T TELL ME YOU'VE FORGOTTEN!
I HAVEN'T! IT'S JUST BEEN SO LONG...
A LAME EXCUSE. CAN IT BE THAT YOU PREFER YOUR KITTY FORM OVER YOUR HUMAN ONE? LOOK AT ME! THIS IS WHO YOU WERE!
WHEN YOU WAKE UP, YOU'RE GOING TO DO WHAT YOU SHOULD HAVE DONE FROM THE BEGINNING! YOU'RE GOING TO TAKE THIS MISTER-KITTY-LITTER AND MAKE IT YOUR OWN! NOW GO!
YOU'RE RIGHT!
I CAN'T BELIEVE I DIDN'T THINK OF IT EARLIER! I COULD BE MAKING BIG BUCKS OFF OF THIS!
POP

TRENDS
TODAY! IN PERSON!
THE CAT WHO INSPIRED MISTER KITTY LITTER!
CHECKOUT
Fitting Room
CD's
SALE
SALE
UH... *WHY* IS NO ONE COMING?
I'M SORRY TO SAY, SALEM, THAT THE FAD HAS *ENDED*. YOU'RE JUST A COUPLE WEEKS TOO LATE, I'M AFRAID.
INK
UGH. NOW I WISH I *NEVER* ASKED FOR SHINJI TO TALK TO HIS UNCLE.
ACTUALLY, THAT HAD NOTHING TO DO WITH IT. IT TURNS OUT HIS UNCLE CAME UP WITH SOME *NEWER*, MORE POPULAR IDEA.
HUH... I WONDER WHAT THAT COULD BE?

BIG SALZ
TODAY! MISS YAPPY PUPPY!
ONE AT A TIME! PLEASE DON T PUSH! YOU'LL ALL HAVE A CHANCE TO CHAT WITH ME BECAUSE I HAVE LOTS OF STUFF TO TALK ABOUT! LIKE ABOUT THAT TIME I MET THAT NICE JAPANESE MAN IN THE PARK! HE SAID I WAS REEEEEAL CUTE AND I SAID, "I KNOW!" AND THEN --
ISN'T THAT THE MOST ADORABLE LITTLE ROBOT YOU'VE EVER SEEN?
YAY!
I KNOW! SHE'S SO MUCH MORE CHARMING THAN THAT MR. CATTY WHATEVER HIS NAME WAS.
WHIMPER
DON'T BE SAD, SALEM. YOU'LL HAVE YOUR DAY AGAIN, I'M SURE OF IT. WHY DON'T WE CATCH A MOVIE? I HEAR THAT THE MISTER KITTY LITTER MOVIE IS PLAYING AT THE DOLLAR THEATRE.
EH, WHAT THE HECK. LET'S DO IT.
FIN!

Chapter 10
Josie
Josie
TANIADELRIO
JIM AMASH

Writer & Artist
TANIA DEL RIO

Inks
JIM AMASH

Colors
JASON JENSEN

Letters
JEFF POWELL

Assistant Editor
MIKE PELLERITO

Editor
VICTOR GORELICK

Editor-In-Chief
RICHARD GOLDWATER

I CAN'T BELIEVE IT!
MY FIRST DOUBLE DATE! THIS PRACTICALLY PROVES THAT HARVEY AND I ARE A COUPLE!
HA HA! TAKE THAT, AMY! AND YOU SAID WE WEREN'T REALLY BOYFRIEND AND GIRLFRIEND!
ERRGH! FOILED AGAIN!
INNER SABRINA
STILL... IT'D BE NICE IF HE PUT HIS ARM AROUND ME OR SOMETHING.

THIS PLACE IS GREAT. YOU GUYS ARE GONNA LOVE IT.
HE KNOWS MORE PLACES IN GREENDALE THAN I DO AND HE DOESN'T EVEN LIVE HERE!
SHORTLY...
LOOKS... INTERESTING.
TRY THIS, LLANDRA, IT'S REALLY GOOD.
MMM, OKAY.
SMAK
WHY CAN'T HARVEY DO THINGS LIKE THAT? I GUESS I'LL HAVE TO BE THE ONE TO INITIATE THINGS!
HARVEY, YOU WANT TO TRY SOME OF MINE?
UH, NO, THAT'S--
ULP!
ARGGGH! IT BURNS!!
OOPS. I FORGOT YOU DON'T LIKE SPICY FOOD.

IT'S A GOOD THING WE GOT MOVIE TICKETS AHEAD OF TIME. WE CAN TAKE OUR TIME GETTING THERE.
HARVEY? ARE YOU OKAY? YOU LOOK KIND OF... PUFFY.
HEH HEH, I THINK THE FOOD DIDN'T AGREE WITH ME. YOU KNOW ME, I'M MORE OF A MEAT AND POTATOES KIND OF GUY.
OOH! JOSIE AND THE PUSSYCATS ARE COMING TO GREENDALE! THOSE CHICKS ARE SO CUTE!
LET'S GET A MOVE ON, SHINJI! WE DON'T WANT TO MISS THE MOVIE!
YANK
OW! BUT I THOUGHT YOU SAID WE HAD PLENTY OF TIME!
"RED LEAVES FALLING". THIS MOVIE SOUNDS ROMANTIC! I HOPE HARVEY HOLDS MY HAND OR SOMETHING.
THIS IS THE STORY OF A SUMMER THAT TURNED TO EARLY FALL.
A SUMMER WHEN RED LEAVES WERE RIPPED FROM THE TREES AND SPIRALED TO THE GROUND IN DEATH.
THEY WERE RED BECAUSE THE VIOLENCE STAINED THEM SO ... IT WAS A SUMMER OF SUFFERING.
I THOUGHT THIS WAS A ROMANCE...

WELL, IT SEEMS THAT HARVEY ISN'T GOING TO MAKE A MOVE. IT'S UP TO ME!
GRAB
GULP!
SO... CLAMMY!
I'M SORRY, SABRINA, I'M JUST NOT FEELING REALLY GOOD. I THINK I NEED TO GO HOME.
WHAT?!
I'M SORRY.
WAIT! I'LL COME WITH YOU!
NO, NO. I JUST NEED TO GET SOME REST. YOU STAY HERE, OKAY?
BUT, HARVEY--
SHHHH! QUIET!

BLAM BLAM BLAM
ARRRRRGGGGHHH!!
SIGH...
I'M SORRY HARVEY HAD TO LEAVE, SABRINA.
S'OKAY. THE DATE WAS PRETTY MUCH OVER, ANYWAY.
OH, THANK GOODNESS! YOU HAVE TO HELP ME OUT!
HUH?
MY NAME'S LUCA--I'M A PHOTOGRAPHER. ONE OF MY MODELS DIDN'T SHOW UP AND I NEED SOMEONE TO STAND IN FOR THIS SHOOT! YOU'RE PERFECT FOR THE JOB!
I AM?
NOT YOU--HIM!

ME?!
YES, YES! A MALE MODEL! YOUR LOOK IS PERFECT, TOO! IT'S A FASHION SHOOT FOR A LOCAL MAGAZINE AND THE PRINTS ARE DUE TOMORROW! PLEASE HELP ME OUT-- YOU'LL BE PAID FOR YOUR TIME!
OKAY, THEN! SOUNDS LIKE FUN!
GREAT, GREAT! COME WITH ME. AND DON'T WORRY IF YOU DON'T HAVE ANY EXPERIENCE. THE GIRLS WILL SHOW YOU HOW TO DO THINGS-- THEY ALL HAVE SEVERAL YEARS OF MODELING EXPERIENCE.
THE GIRLS?!
SORRY, LADIES! DUTY CALLS! I'LL CATCH YOU GUYS LATER!
FUME
THE NERVE!
SHORTLY...

ALRIGHT, THIS AD IS GOING TO BE FOR SOME NEW MEN'S CLOTHING, BUT THE GIRLS ARE GOING TO BE POSING WITH YOU TO CALL MORE ATTENTION TO YOUR OUTFIT.
SWEET.
NOW, DON'T BE NERVOUS. JUST LET THE GIRLS GATHER AROUND YOU LIKE SO AND TRY TO ACT NATURAL. COOL. IN CONTROL.
WOW.
HE'S A NATURAL.
EXCELLENT, EXCELLENT! HOLD IT!
CLICK

ROGUE
WILD SPIRIT: WE CHAT WITH SHINJI YAMAGI, GREENDALE'S HOTTEST MODEL
RUGGED OUTDOOR DAY TRIPS
Kayak Review
LOLITA
DRESSING UP WITH SHINJI YAMAGI
MAKEUP THAT LASTS ALL DAY
GOTHIC GARDENING
Tween
Magazine
Is Shinji your type? Find out with our quiz!
BACKSTABBING BEST FRIENDS? HOW TO COPE
POP ARTISTS OF THE YEAR

GREENDALE HIGH...
SHINJI'S SO CUTE!
HE SPOKE TO ME ONCE!
HOW COME HE'S NEVER AT SCHOOL ANYMORE?
DUH, BECAUSE HE'S FAMOUS NOW!
I WONDER IF HE HAS A GIRLFRIEND?
AS A MATTER OF FACT, HE DOES!
WAH!
SLAM
SCARY!
SHE'S JUST BITTER. I HEARD THAT SHE HAS A MAJOR CRUSH ON SHINJI BUT HE WANTS NOTHING TO DO WITH HER.
TCH I CAN SEE WHY!
MAN, WHAT'S GOTTEN INTO SHINJI? EVER SINCE HIS MODELING CAREER HAS TAKEN OFF, HE'S HARDLY SHOWN UP FOR SCHOOL. I THINK IT'S TIME FOR AN INTERVENTION!
NEW

I DON'T KNOW, SABRINA. IS IT REALLY *OUR* BUSINESS?
LLANDRA, YOU'RE HIS *GIRLFRIEND!* OF *COURSE* IT'S YOUR BUSINESS! HE'S *DITCHING* SCHOOL, DON'T YOU THINK THAT'S A BIG DEAL?
I DON'T WANT HIM TO BE *MAD* AT ME... I MEAN IT'S BAD ENOUGH THAT I *HARDLY* SEE HIM ANYMORE BECAUSE HE'S SO BUSY. AND I'M *ALREADY* UPSET THAT HE SPENDS HIS DAYS SURROUNDED BY BEAUTIFUL GIRLS!
ALL THE *MORE* REASON TO TALK TO HIM. WE NEED TO REMIND HIM OF *REALITY!*
SHORTLY...
I CAN'T TALK LONG, GIRLS. I HAVE TO BE AT A *SHOOT* IN ABOUT HALF AN HOUR.
SHINJI, THIS IS *IMPORTANT*.
WE'RE *CONCERNED* THAT YOU HAVEN'T BEEN COMING TO SCHOOL! I *KNOW* YOU'RE BUSY MODELING, BUT YOU'RE GOING TO *FAIL* IF YOU DON'T START DOING YOUR SCHOOLWORK!
SO?
SO?!

THIS IS THE BEGINNING OF MY *CAREER!* I ACTUALLY HAVE A *JOB* NOW! I DON'T SEE HOW SLAVING AWAY AT CHEMISTRY AND ENGLISH LIT IS GOING TO HELP ME NOW. MODELING IS WHAT I PLAN TO DO UNTIL I'M *TOO OLD* AND BY THEN I'LL HAVE ENOUGH IN THE BANK TO LIVE *COMFORTABLY*.
SO YOU DON'T *CARE* ABOUT ANYTHING NOW THAT YOU'RE A *BIG TIME MODEL?*
YOU DON'T CARE ABOUT YOUR *EDUCATION* AND YOU DON'T CARE ABOUT *US!* ABOUT *ME...*
OF *COURSE* I CARE ABOUT YOU!
OOPS, GOTTA GET GOING!
WE'LL TALK LATER.

CHARM SCHOOL...
LOOK WHO IT IS!
SHINJI! YOU'RE AT SCHOOL!
YEAH, IT'S A BIT OF AN ESCAPE FOR ME. I CAN'T GO ANYWHERE IN THE MORTAL REALM WITHOUT GIRLS FOLLOWING ME AROUND. BUT NONE OF THE CHICKS HERE KNOW ABOUT MY MODELING SO I CAN REMEMBER WHAT IT'S LIKE TO BE A REGULAR PERSON AND NOT A SUPERSTAR.
FULL OF HIMSELF, ISN'T HE?
ANYWAY, THE MAIN REASON I CAME WAS TO GIVE YOU GUYS TICKETS TO THE UPCOMING JOSIE AND THE PUSSYCATS SHOW IN GREENDALE. IT TURNS OUT I'LL BE MODELING WITH THEM TOMORROW, ISN'T THAT SWEET? YOU GUYS CAN TAG ALONG AND SEE ME WORK MY MAGIC ON THE MODELING SCENE!

HE NEXT DAY...
I CAN'T WAIT TO MEET JOSIE AND THE PUSSYCATS! THEY'RE SO CUTE!
SO I'VE HEARD.
WOAH, WOAH, WOAH. ARE YOU THE MODEL?
YEAH. WELL, I AM, ANYWAY.
THEN WHO ARE THEY?
MY FRIENDS. THEY WANT TO SEE ME MODEL.
FRIEND?
SORRY, DUDE. THIS IS A CLOSED SET. YOUR FRIENDS ARE GONNA HAVE TO WAIT OUTSIDE.
AW MAN, I'M REALLY SORRY, GIRLS. WELL, AT LEAST WE CAN ALL GO TO THE CONCERT, RIGHT?
JERK!
WHY DIDN'T HE TELL HIM I WAS HIS GIRLFRIEND? I BET I WOULD HAVE BEEN LET IN, THEN.

I BET HE DOESN'T WANT ANYONE TO KNOW HE HAS A GIRLFRIEND. THAT WAY HE CAN FLIRT WITH ALL THE GIRLS HE WANTS!
NO, LLANDRA. I'M SURE HE'S NOT LIKE THAT...
...I THINK. WHAT IF LLANDRA'S RIGHT?
IF SHINJI EVER HURT LLANDRA I'D--
ERRRGH
SABRINA? LET'S GO.
INVISIBILITY? IT'S TOO RISKY.
NO! IF YOU'RE WORRIED ABOUT SHINJI, WE CAN STILL SEE WHAT HE'S DOING. WITH MAGIC!
NOPE. WE'LL JUST TURN MY EYESHADOW INTO SPYSHADOW!
ZAP

IT'S SO NICE TO MEET YOU LADIES! YOU'RE EVEN MORE BEAUTIFUL IN PERSON!
GIGGLE
HA HA, I KNOW YOUR TYPE! I'M KEEPING MY DISTANCE!
DON'T BE MEAN, VAL!
IT'S ONLY BEEN 10 MINUTES AND HE'S ALREADY FLIRTING!
HE'S JUST TRYING TO BE CHARMING. YOU'LL SEE, WHEN IT COMES DOWN TO IT, HE'S A FAITHFUL GUY.
THESE AREN'T REAL, ARE THEY? I'M ALLERGIC TO CATS, YOU KNOW!
REALLY?
IF I SAY NO, WILL YOU STAY CLOSE TO ME?
GIGGLE
OKAY, WE'RE READY TO BEGIN!
TIME TO WORK!

Josie

AT FIRST HE SEEMED LIKE HE WAS ALL FUN AND GAMES, BUT SHINJI REALLY TAKES THIS SERIOUSLY.
Josie
UNFORTUNATELY, HE'S A BIT OF A DIVA.
I'M GOING TO NEED SOME WATER OVER HERE. DON'T FORGET--TWO ICE CUBES AND A LEMON SLICE! OH, AND NO TAP WATER. BUT YOU KNEW THAT.
UH, YEAH. BE RIGHT BACK.
MAKEUP! I THINK I NEED A LITTLE TOUCH UP! THE POWDER FEELS A LITTLE THICK AND IT'S GETTING IN MY EYES! MY HANDS COULD USE SOME MORE LOTION, TOO! SERIOUSLY, WHERE IS EVERYONE? I SHOULDN'T EVEN HAVE TO ASK!
MODELS. THEY'RE ALL THE SAME. BUT THIS ONE'S EVEN HARDER TO WORK WITH THAN KATY KEENE!
SHINJI'S ACTING LIKE A SPOILED BRAT! I HARDLY EVEN RECOGNIZE HIM ANYMORE.

ATER...
ALRIGHT! THAT'S A WRAP! THANKS, EVERYONE!
PHEW! NOW THAT THAT'S OVER WITH, IT'S TIME TO PAR-TAY!
WHAT?
I KNOW TONS OF POPULAR SPOTS AROUND GREENDALE AND THE NIGHT IS STILL YOUNG! LET'S GET OUT THERE AND SHOW THE TOWN HOW ROCK STARS DO THINGS!
OOH! YOU KNOW ROCK STARS?
SORRY, SHINJI, BUT WE HAVE SCHOOLWORK TO DO. WE HAVE TO MEET WITH OUR TUTOR NOW.
SCHOOLWORK? YOU'RE JOKING, RIGHT?
WELL, SINCE WE'RE ALWAYS ON THE ROAD WE DON'T GO TO A REGULAR HIGH SCHOOL. BUT WE STILL TAKE LESSONS SO WE DON'T MISS OUT ON ANYTHING.
YEAH, WE DON'T WANT TO GROW UP NOT BEING VERY SMART!
I DON'T GET IT. WHY BOTHER, RIGHT? I MEAN, WE'RE YOUNG AND POPULAR! WE SHOULD MAKE THE MOST OF IT NOW!
YEAH, EXCEPT ONE DAY WE'RE NOT GOING TO BE YOUNG AND POPULAR ANYMORE. WE'LL NEED TO FIND REAL JOBS AND THAT'S GOING TO BE IMPOSSIBLE UNLESS WE FINISH SCHOOL!
I WANT TO BE A VET!

BUT AFTER MY HOMEWORK'S DONE, MAYBE YOU AND ME CAN GO OUT. *TOGETHER*, I MEAN. LIKE A *DATE!*
GASP!
SORRY, MELODY. YOU'RE CUTE BUT I HAVE TO BE *HONEST*. I HAVE A *GIRLFRIEND* SO THAT MEANS *NO MORE* DATES FOR ME! UNLESS THEY'RE WITH *HER,* OF COURSE.
AWWW... YOU *ARE* ALLERGIC TO CATS, HUH?
SEE? SHINJI'S TRUE TO YOU. I KNEW HE WOULD BE.
I HAVE TO ADMIT, I'M A LITTLE SURPRISED. I DIDN'T REALIZE SHINJI WAS *SO SERIOUS* ABOUT LLANDRA.
GOOD FOR HER...

CONCERT NIGHT...
JOSIE & The Pussycats™
AWESOME SHOW, RIGHT?!
YEAH! WHAT'S WRONG WITH SHINJI, THOUGH? HE LOOKS A LITTLE BUMMED!
HE QUIT THE MODELING BUSINESS. HE'S GOING BACK TO SCHOOL.
HE QUIT?! HE COULD HAVE FOUND A WAY TO DO BOTH!
I DON'T KNOW THE WHOLE STORY, BUT APPARENTLY HE QUIT DURING A BEACH SHOOT. THE PHOTOGRAPHER WANTED HIM TO TAKE OFF HIS SHIRT AND SHINJI FLIPPED OUT. I DON'T KNOW WHY, AND I'M NOT ABOUT TO ASK. HE SEEMS PRETTY UPSET ABOUT IT.
IT'S GOOD TO HAVE YOU BACK, SHINJI!

SO IT'S OVER. I'M NO LONGER A BIG SHOT MODEL. I GUESS I SHOULD BE HAPPY. IT WAS ALL LIKE A CRAZY DREAM AND A BIG HEADACHE ALL AT ONCE.
THAT DARN PHOTOGRAPHER! WHY DID HE HAVE TO ASK ME TO TAKE MY SHIRT OFF! I WASN'T READY FOR IT!
THIS THING... IT'S COST ME EVERYTHING. FIRST MY CHILDHOOD, MY DIGNITY, THEN MY FIRST REAL JOB. WHAT NEXT, MY FRIENDS?
I CAN'T HIDE IT. IT'S ALWAYS THERE.
END!

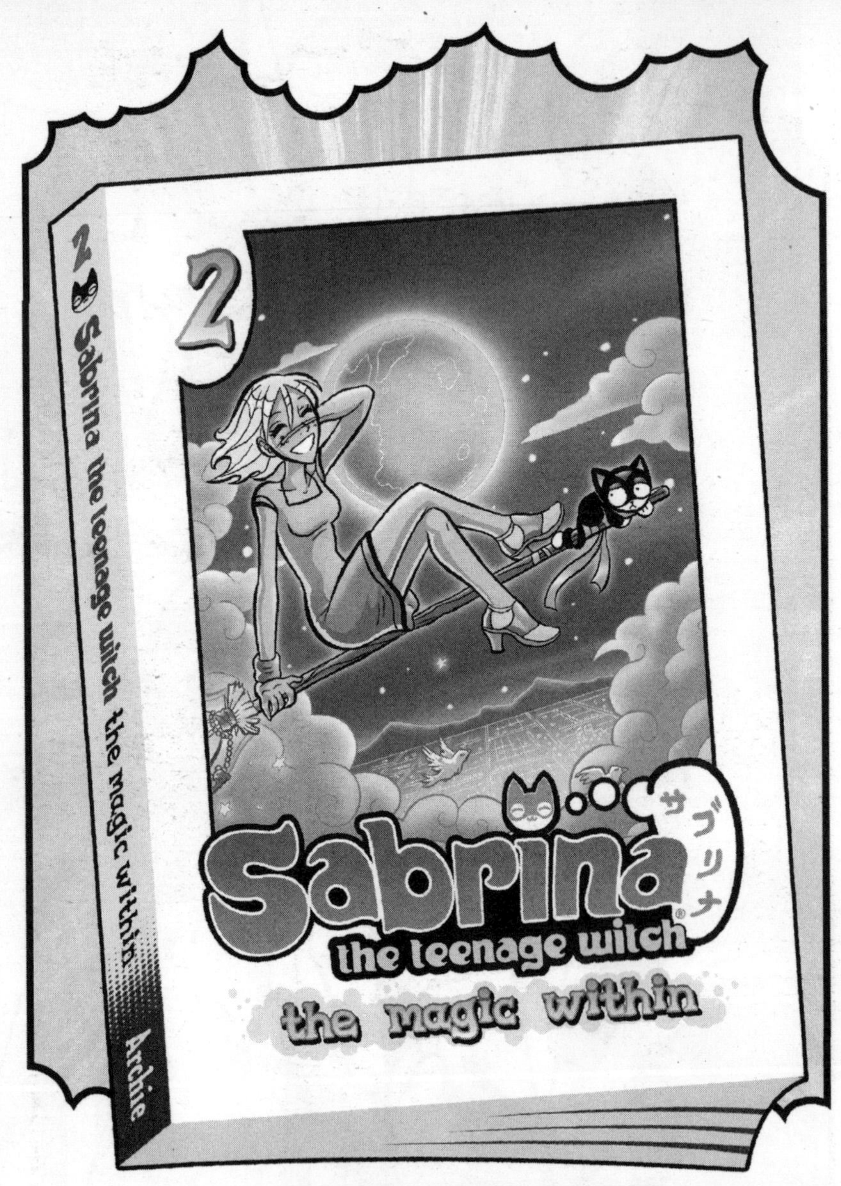

Now, check out a sneak peek of what's next!

Wish You Were Here
Writer & Artist Tania Del Rio Inks Jim Amash
Colors Jason Jensen Letters Jeff Powell
Assistant Editor Mike Pellerito Editor Victor Gorelick
Editor-In-Chief Richard Goldwater
TICK-TOCK
TICK TOCK...
TREMBLE
CLICK
WE'RE FREEE! SUMMER BREAK IS HERE!
SABRINA, THAT CLOCK IS 10 MINUTES FAST. PLEASE SIT DOWN SO I CAN FINISH WRITING YOUR SUMMER HOMEWORK ON THE BOARD.
TWO WHOLE MONTHS! WHAT DO YOU WANT TO DO THIS SUMMER?
UH...

WE CAN GO SEE MOVIES! OR MAYBE CAMPING FOR A COUPLE DAYS! OR WE COULD JUST HANG OUT AT HOME AND PLAY VIDEOGAMES TOGETHER! THERE'S TONS OF THINGS WE COULD DO!
UH...
ACTUALLY, SABRINA, I'M GOING AWAY FOR THE SUMMER.
AWAY?! WHERE?
I'M GOING WITH MY FAMILY TO VISIT MY RELATIVES. I'LL BE GONE MOST OF THE SUMMER.
JUST MY LUCK. ALL THIS TIME OFF AND I WON'T EVEN GET TO SPEND IT WITH HARVEY... I'LL BE STUCK BEING THE THIRD WHEEL AROUND SHINJI AND LLANDRA.
WHEN DO YOU LEAVE? MAYBE WE CAN GO ON A DATE OR SOMETHING BEFORE YOU GO...
ACTUALLY... I LEAVE TOMORROW MORNING.
TOMORROW?! THEN, CAN WE DO SOMETHING TONIGHT? I WON'T BE ABLE TO SEE YOU FOR TWO WHOLE MONTHS!
I KNOW, SORRY. BUT I'M GOING TO BE TOO BUSY PACKING MY STUFF. DON'T WORRY, THOUGH. THE TIME WILL GO BY FAST.
WELL, CAN I STOP BY TOMORROW MORNING TO SEE YOU OFF?
I DON'T THINK THAT'S A GOOD IDEA... THINGS ARE GOING TO BE CRAZY WITH US TRYING TO GET TO THE AIRPORT ON TIME.
SO... WE HAVE TO SAY GOODBYE HERE? NOW?
YEAH... I GUESS SO.

-SNIFF- ALRIGHT THEN. I'LL SEE YOU NEXT TERM.
NOT HERE, SABRINA. SOMEONE MIGHT SEE US!
I'LL KEEP IN TOUCH, OKAY? YOU'LL HAVE PLENTY OF FUN WITHOUT ME, YOU'LL SEE!
THE SUMMER DRAMA BEGINS ALREADY? WHAT'S WRONG NOW?
HARVEY'S GOING AWAY FOR THE WHOLE SUMMER. I DON'T KNOW WHAT TO DO...
DO WHAT YOU DO EVERY SUMMER: GO SWIMMING, GO SHOPPING, CATCH UP ON YOUR MANGA. YOU DON'T NEED THAT LOSER AROUND TO KEEP YOU HAPPY!
SALEM! HARVEY IS NOT A LOSER! BUT YOU'RE RIGHT. I HAVE PLENTY OF THINGS TO DO. I'M GOING TO HAVE A FUN SUMMER, WITH OR WITHOUT HARVEY!
IN FACT, I HAVE TONS OF THINGS TO DO! I DON'T EVEN KNOW IF I'D HAVE TIME TO HANG OUT WITH HARVEY EVEN IF HE WAS HERE!
THAT'S THE SPIRIT!
To be continued in...
Sabrina サブリナ
the teenage witch
the magic within
volume 2!
Available in stores June 2013!

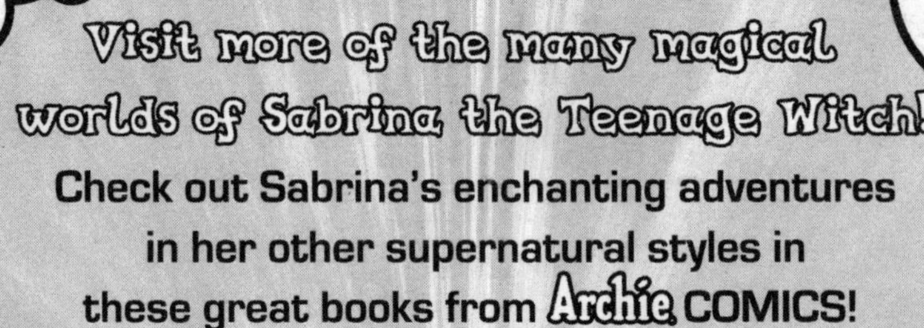

The Magic of Sabrina the Teenage Witch

Earlier stories with Shinji, Llandra, Harvey and Salem!

ISBN:
978-1-879794-75-7

Sabrina: Animated

More fun Sabrina stories based on the hit cartoon show!

ISBN:
978-1-879794-80-1

Archie Meets KISS

One of Sabrina's spells brings KISS to Riverdale to fight fun-draining monsters!

ISBN:
978-1-936975-04-4

The Best of Archie Comics Books 1 & 2

70 years of laughs in two convenient, hilarious packages containing several Sabrina stories, including her first appearance and more!

ISBN:
978-1-879794-84-9

ISBN:
978-1-936975-20-4

FIND THESE AND MORE GREAT ARCHIE BOOKS AT COMIC SHOPS, BOOKSTORES, AND ARCHIECOMICS.COM!